Hoofbeats
on the Trail

෯

BOOK 3
in *The Ally O'Connor Adventures*

Hoofbeats
on the Trail

Mark Littleton

Baker Books

A Division of Baker Book House Co
Grand Rapids, Michigan 49516

© 2002 by Mark Littleton

Published by Baker Books
a division of Baker Book House Company
P.O. Box 6287, Grand Rapids, MI 49516-6287

Printed in the United States of America

Library of Congress Cataloging-in-Publication Data

Littleton, Mark R., 1950–
   Hoofbeats on the trail / Mark Littleton.
       p.   cm. (Ally O'Connor adventures ; 3)
   Summary: When fourteen-year-old horse enthusiast Ally meets
Jeff and discovers that he is suspected of stealing from neighborhood
homes, her would-be boyfriend Nick worries that Jeff will steal Ally's
affections as well.
   ISBN 0-8010-6427-9 (pbk.)
   [1. Horses—Fiction. 2. Christian life—Fiction. 3. Mystery and
detective stories.] I. Title. II. Series.
PZ7 .L7364 Ho 2002
[Fic]—dc21
                                             2002009128

For current information about all releases from Baker Book House, visit our
web site:
                http://www.bakerbooks.com

Contents

Contents

Cast of Characters

Ally O' Connor: A fun-spirited, fourteen-year-old eighth grader with a zest for life and a love of horses.

Nick Parker: Ally's tall, blond, teasing friend, also fourteen and an eighth grader, who has an obvious crush on Ally.

Jeff Reynolds: A boy Ally's age who has jet-black hair and talks and behaves at times like a Southern gent right out of *Gone with the Wind*, or a medieval-knight wannabe.

Nestor Coombs, known as "Coombsie": A friend of Jeff's who lives in the woods. He has a long gray beard and twinkly green eyes, and he wears clothes made out of deer-skin and smokes a pipe. He loves to tell stories, and is an amazing violinist.

Barbara "Babs" Kruck: Jeff's aunt (the sister of Jeff's absent father); she is single, tall, thin, and attractive.

Molly Parker: Nick's earnest little sister, an eleven-year-old blonde, with freckles and a pure heart.

Mrs. O'Connor: Ally's mom, who has the same blue eyes and auburn hair as her daughter.

Mr. O'Connor: Ally's father, a tall, lean man with bright green eyes and a walruslike mustache.

Mrs. Hanson: An elderly woman with rosy cheeks and a friendly air. She has a horse farm.

Snowbird: One of Mrs. Hanson's horses that Ally has ridden.

Thunder: A stallion at the Hanson horse farm.

Lucky: The horse Nick rides from the Hanson farm.

Mr. Bell: A man in the neighborhood who tells the O'Connors of rental homes that are being broken into and trashed.

One

A Crossing of Evergreens

Ally O'Connor and her friend Nick Parker stepped onto the dirt road. Its center was covered with a down of grass, but it looked well-traveled.

"It's just up a ways," Ally said, peering through the trees. Ally had discovered a horse farm less than a mile from her home. The Hanson family ran it, and Ally had already ridden one of the horses, Snowbird.

"C'mon, Nick." Ally, impatient, started down the road. "It's the coolest place. They'll let us ride anytime. They need to exercise the horses a lot, and they just don't have the people to do it."

"Just what I always wanted to do," Nick said. "Exercise horses."

"Oh, don't be a foof. Wait till you see Thunder. He's the most beautiful horse I ever saw."

"Even better than the wild mustangs at Corolla?"

"Those *were* pretty special," Ally said, her eyes twinkling as she remembered their adventure to save the wild horses around their vacation home. "But this is a horse for riding—and you know how I love to ride."

"The queen of horsewomen, that's you." Nick scrunched his spiky blond hair and plodded after Ally.

"You know, you could smile a little," she chastised, half-teasing. "It wouldn't hurt your face."

"I don't like the idea of climbing up on a big horse and then being pitched off into the dirt."

"Oh, you know how to ride," Ally said, pushing back her own auburn hair. She grinned and patted Nick on the shoulder. "You just have to learn some of the more advanced things, like galloping without your hand on the pommel. Anyway, I'm a pro. I'll teach you everything."

"Thanks a lot." Nick feigned deep gratitude. "I guess we'll have to shovel out the stalls and everything. Maybe even find an ancient jewel in the horse dung, is that it?"

"Oh, it won't be that bad. Anyway, you like the smell, don't you?"

"Ha, ha. Will you quit with the jokes!"

"Okay, fella, in a little mood today, aren't you?" Ally teased.

"I keep thinking it's over four hundred days before I can take you out on our first date."

"Remember that Jacob loved Rachel so much that seven years seemed like a day."

Nick laughed. "I don't love you that much."

"Really now?" Ally struck a model's pose. "You don't think I'm beautiful enough?"

"You're beautiful enough. But I don't want to wait four hundred days or seven years."

"So think of today as a date."

"That's what I keep telling myself."

The road curved to the left up ahead. Ally was trying to see beyond it when she heard the pounding of hooves. She stopped. "Someone's coming!"

Nick glanced to his right and left as if to find a hiding place.

Seconds later, a horse came into view with a rider who appeared to be Nick and Ally's age, fourteen or so. He thundered toward them, grabbing a branch of a pine tree. He broke it off and headed straight toward Ally and Nick. Nick jumped from the path to the side of the road, tugging Ally with him.

The rider pulled up his horse fast, then with a grandiose gesture said, "Welcome to the neighborhood." With a huge grin, he handed Ally the sprig of pine. "For you, milady."

Ally twirled the sprig between her fingers, unsure of this boy whose jet-black hair shone in the afternoon sunlight. "Uh, thanks," she stammered.

"Sorry, nothing for you," the boy said to Nick.

"Fine with me," Nick said. "But who—"

Before he could finish the question, the rider kicked the brown thoroughbred's flank. "Away!" he cried. The horse reared and then dashed forward, disappearing around a bend.

Ally was speechless, but Nick said, "Looks like you have an admirer."

"Who on earth is he?" Ally finally exclaimed, giving the sprig a sniff, then stuffing it into her shirt pocket, where a piece of it stuck out like the head of a small green doll.

"What's up with the twig? Is that supposed to be a present or something?" Nick said with a snort.

"Oh, be quiet. You never gave me a flower, let alone a freshly plucked plume of pine."

"Hey, good alliteration!" Nick noticed. "We learned about using words that start with the same letter in English last year."

"I learned about it from Mom five years ago."

"That's because she's a writer."

"As I will be one day, in addition to an artist and an equestrian giant among women."

"You're going to be a giant? I'd love to see that. Which will be longer, your legs or your arms?"

Ally gave him a look of mock disgust. "I think you need to go to your cave, Nick."

"I don't have a cave."

"We'll find you one."

Nick laughed as Ally shook her head and turned to walk on. "We'll get to the bottom of this mysterious horseman in a few minutes. That was one of Mrs. Hanson's horses, I'm sure of it."

Breaking into a jog, Ally and Nick rounded the bend and saw the farmhouse up ahead. In another minute, they stood at the front door.

Mrs. Hanson, an elderly woman with rosy cheeks and a friendly air, answered. "Back so soon, Ally?" she asked.

"We just wanted to go riding," Ally said. "This is my friend, Nick Parker. I'd like to teach him some of the basics. And exercise the horses, of course."

"They do need it."

Behind her, Ally heard the clattering of hooves. She turned to see the mysterious boy on the brown thoroughbred.

"Oh, have you met our new stable hand?" Mrs. Hanson said.

Ally's eyes narrowed. "Sort of."

"He fancies himself a knight in shining armor, I think," Mrs. Hanson said, her eyes bright. "We just hired him. He lives down the road."

"What's his name?"

The boy and the horse disappeared into the barn. Mrs. Hanson said, "Come on, I'll introduce you."

She stepped off the porch of the farmhouse and led Ally and Nick back to the barn. There they found Jeff unsaddling the thoroughbred and cooling him down.

"Jeff," Mrs. Hanson said. "This is Ally O'Connor and her friend. What did you say your name was, son?"

"Nick. Nick Parker," Nick replied.

"Well, Jeff, this is your lucky day. You won't have to give all the horses some exercise, since these two will help you out. And I don't have to pay them a dime. Ally, Nick, this is Jeff Reynolds."

Jeff wiped off his hands and stepped forward. He was a bit taller than Ally, slim and sharp-nosed. Ally could tell Nick was jealous, so she decided to forget about the sprig of pine and be on her best behavior.

"Pleased to meet you," Ally said, shaking Jeff's hand.

Jeff bowed slightly, as if he'd just stepped out of *Gone with the Wind*. "I think I've seen you before," he said. "Was it holding a piece of pine bough?"

Nick stuck out his hand. "I'm Nick. Glad to meet you."

Jeff took Nick's hand and shook it vigorously.

"Hey," Nick said, pulling back. "I'm not a washing machine."

"Sorry," Jeff said. "I get enthusiastic sometimes."

"We'll be glad to exercise a couple of the horses, Mrs. Hanson," Ally said. "I'd like to take Snowbird if he hasn't been exercised yet. Who should we give to Nick?"

"I'd say Blackberry," Jeff interjected.

Ally eyed him. "I was asking Mrs. Hanson."

Jeff's face went red, and he turned to continue brushing down the tall thoroughbred. But Nick grinned as if he'd just won a victory.

Mrs. Hanson walked to the stall across from the thoroughbred's. "I'd say Lucky should be pretty easy on him."

"Thanks," Ally said. "Let me show him how to blanket and saddle the horses, and we'll get going."

"I'll be glad to help," Jeff said from his stall.

"We'll be fine," Ally said, suddenly not sure why she was acting as if she didn't like Jeff. Maybe it was the whole pine tree thing. She wasn't looking for some knight in shining armor, after all.

But she couldn't deny that there was something about him that she liked.

Suddenly, she felt Nick's eyes on her. "We'll be fine," Ally said again, then glanced at Jeff. The boy was watching her over the top rail of the stall. *Oh well*, she thought. *I'm only fourteen. I can't date till I'm sixteen.*

She wasn't going to think about any boy till then.

Two

Invaders

Mrs. O'Connor met Nick and Ally at the door that night. "Have you heard anything about houses being broken into in the area?" she asked.

"No," Ally said and glanced at Nick. He shook his head. "What happened?"

"Well, we'll find out in about five minutes," Mrs. O'Connor said, turning to the dinner cooking on the stove. The doorbell rang and over her shoulder she asked Ally, "Would you get that?"

Ally was already there. A well-dressed man with a mustache and bright blue eyes peered inside. "Hi, I'm Mr. Bell," he said. "Is your mom here? I phoned her a few minutes ago to let her know I was on my way."

Nick excused himself to head home for his own dinner as Mr. Bell joined the O'Connors in the living room.

Ally's mom and dad sat down beside her on their big leather couch as Mr. Bell took the easy chair opposite. "It's really very simple," he said. "Some rentals down the street have been broken into and busted up. We think it might be a kid, or maybe several kids."

"What makes you think it's kids?" Mr. O'Conner asked.

15

"Well, they're stealing mainly electronic equipment. But the worst thing is that they're tearing up the houses inside— pure, plain vandalism for no reason we can figure."

Mr. O'Connor unknotted his tie. "Do you think our place is in danger?"

"I suppose anyone's is," Mr. Bell mused, frowning. "Whoever's doing this is watching the houses rather carefully, and they're hitting up places when the residents are out of town."

"You said rentals?" Mrs. O'Connor asked.

"Yes." Mr. Bell cleared his throat. "Well, so far all of the houses broken into have been rentals—mostly furnished rentals, so it's not a loss so much for the people who are renting as people like me who own the places. Not an immediate cost, anyway. If this keeps up, we're going to have to charge more for security."

"Do you think the robbers or whoever know they're rentals?" Ally asked, her investigative skills clicking into full throb.

"No." Mr. Bell glanced around uncomfortably. "Rentals just happen to be the ones that have been hit. Maybe it's because the rentals are vacant at times, between tenants. Two of them were hit when there were no renters living on the premises."

"Interesting," Ally whispered to herself.

"How so?" Mr. O'Connor asked, focusing intently on his daughter.

"Nothing really, I guess," Ally thought aloud. "Just kind of strange. I wouldn't think rental furniture would be in that good of shape. Or the electronic equipment."

Mr. Bell nodded. "Can't figure that one out."

"Aren't the police involved?" Mrs. O'Connor said, standing. "I've got to check on the oven, so I'll be going in a moment."

"I didn't mean to stay long," Mr. Bell said. "I just wanted to let you know what's going on and to allay your fears.

Don't go out of town for a lengthy period of time is what I can suggest at this point. Are you going anywhere?"

"Not for awhile," Mr. O'Connor said.

Mr. Bell got up. "Let me know—or the police—if you notice anything strange or any kids hanging around." He held out his hand.

Mr. O'Connor shook it, and Mrs. O'Connor thanked Mr. Bell and left the living room.

"And your name?" Mr. Bell smiled as Ally held the door.

"Ally."

"Nice name. I have a niece with that name. Well, good day." Mr. Bell walked out the door, and Ally closed it behind him.

"We'd better leave the lights on any nights we go out," Mr. O'Connor told Ally.

"And I'll keep an eye out," she answered, troubled.

"First, though," Mr. O'Connor said, knowing how his daughter could fret over things, "let's eat."

The next afternoon, Ally stepped outside for a power walk, her latest way to build her stamina and develop her leg muscles. She was well down the street when she heard the clopping of horse's hooves on the macadam. She turned around. *Jeff! How does he always sneak up like that?*

"Hey, want a ride?" he called.

Since it was late summer, he wore just jeans, a shirt, and a baseball cap. He drew up next to Ally. "We could run through the fields on that farm down the street."

"Oh, the people that lived there were friends of mine," Ally said, referring to her friend Sarah and her mom. "They had some problems, and the house burned down, along with the barn. No one lives there right now."

"I know," Jeff said, grinning down at Ally. "It gives me a chance to run Snowbird here." He held out his hand.

Ally hesitated, then grabbed it, and Jeff pulled her up easily behind him. "You're light," he said.

"All ninety pounds of me," Ally answered.

Ally got settled behind the western saddle and put her arms around Jeff's waist.

A moment later, Jeff kicked the big horse. "Heigh-ho!"

Snowbird jolted into a trot, almost knocking Ally off. Her teeth seemed to rattle in her head. "Can you speed it up?" Ally said, leaning around Jeff. "I'm having my teeth fall out here."

Jeff grinned. "Sure." He kicked the horse again and said, "Go, Snowbird!"

Seconds later, they were cantering down the street past the rental houses. The afternoon breeze felt good on Ally's face.

"So where do you live, Jeff?" she called over the thundering of the hooves.

"Across the bridge at the end of your street, on the other side of the development."

"What's your dad do?"

"I live with my aunt."

This revelation quieted Ally a moment as she mulled over what this might mean. She pushed back instinctive caution. "Where are your parents?" she ventured.

"My mom's dead. My dad is . . . not around. I live with my Aunt Barbara—she goes by Babs, but I call her Barbara. I can't get used to Babs. It sounds weird to me."

Ally shifted her weight slightly to get into a better position. "Is your aunt your father's sister?"

"Yeah. She's not married. Never has been. She's a little strange."

"Really?"

"Well, in a good way, I guess. But I don't like all her rules. Or her Jesus stuff."

"She's a Christian?"

"Yeah. Big time."

18

"I'm a Christian too."

"Really." Jeff didn't sound pleased. He whacked the reins on the horse's neck, and she pitched into a full canter.

Ally thought she'd like to meet Jeff's aunt. She sounded fascinating, to say nothing of the fact that she was of like faith. As they rumbled along, Ally prayed that she might get a chance to witness to Jeff when the time was right.

They reached the end of the street, and Jeff pulled up Snowbird. He led the horse down into the trees to a narrow trail just wide enough for horse and rider. A moment later, they came out in the cornfield of the Matthews's farm.

Jeff found a line between the furrows and steered the horse through the corn, walking.

"So where are we going now?" Ally asked.

"Wherever you want," Jeff answered, his dark hair riffling in the breeze. Ally's hair blew across her face, and she let go with one hand to brush it out of her eyes.

"Thick forests with trolls under rocks. Meadows with deer that will eat out of your hand. Castles with moats and . . . "

"Okay, okay," she said laughing but enjoying Jeff's imaginative answer. "Just take me for a little ride to the farmhouse and back."

They reached the edge of the corn, and Jeff stopped Snowbird for a moment. "I always wondered what happened to that house."

"I'll tell you about it someday."

"I used to see the owner on this big brown thoroughbred."

"Colonel," Ally said. "He was wonderful. He's somewhere in New Jersey now, I think. Sarah and her mother had to sell him."

"Too bad. He looked like a real racehorse." Jeff was silent for a moment, then said, "Hold onto your hat" as he kicked the horse. Moments later they were galloping around the edge of the property.

"Don't . . . fall . . . off!" he called.

Snowbird's gallop was smooth, with just the bumping and thumping of her hooves disturbing the quiet of the afternoon.

When they had circled around the burned-out farmhouse and barn, Jeff led Snowbird back into the rows of corn and out to Ally's street. He stopped in front of her house, and Ally climbed down.

"Whew! That was nice," she said.

"Why don't you come on over to my aunt's house tonight? We can play a game or something."

Ally glanced at her house. "I'll have to ask my mom."

"That's okay. Your friend Nick too. Why don't you both come over?"

"I'll give him a call. What's your phone number?"

Jeff reached into a pocket, dug out a slip of paper, and pulled a pen from his back pocket. He wrote down his number and handed it to her with a wink. "I just have to take Snowbird back and will be home in about half an hour."

"I'll call," Ally promised as Jeff clucked Snowbird up the street. She turned to enter the house, then suddenly stopped. *How did Jeff know this is my house?*

"Another mystery about him," she said aloud as she reached the door. She turned back to see Jeff disappear from sight through the covered bridge at the end of the street. *Maybe Jeff's not so bad after all,* she thought. *At least if Nick's with me, it will be all right. In any case,* Ally brightened, *I want to meet Jeff's aunt.*

"Mom," she called from the foyer. "Can I go somewhere tonight?"

Three

Games and Something More

"So he took you on the horse?" Mrs. O'Connor asked Ally, who was filling in her mom on her adventure with Jeff.

"It was fun," she said, looking to Nick, who'd come by the house that evening with his little sister, Molly. Their parents, the Parkers, and Ally's folks had planned an evening out together, and the kids typically ended up at the O'Connors' when their parents went out. This night, Ally had asked Mrs. O'Connor to give them permission to visit Jeff and his aunt. But first Mrs. O'Connor wanted to know what kind of boy Jeff was.

Ally looked at her mom. "Jeff's a little . . . different."

Nick scoffed. "He thinks he's Sir Lancelot." He took a bite of the frozen pizza Mrs. O'Connor had made for the kids.

Molly, who was eleven and just starting to think of boys— but more about storybook heroes—flashed Ally a hopeful look. "I have to meet this guy."

Mrs. O'Connor put another piece of pizza on Nick's plate. "I think I need to meet his parents before any of you start hanging around him."

"He lives with his aunt," Ally said. "His mother is dead, and his dad is . . . well, kind of a mystery."

"Well, where is his dad?" Mrs. O'Connor said, looking somewhat alarmed.

"Jeff didn't say."

"What's the big deal about this guy, anyways?" Nick said. "Who cares?"

"Look," Ally replied, folding her arms over her chest, "if you don't want to go over to Jeff's house, just say so. I'm not dragging you along if you're going to act like that."

Mrs. O'Connor threw her daughter a "what's this?" look, eyebrows raised.

"Well, I'm trying to get Nick to be friends with this guy," Ally said in answer to the look. "Who knows? Maybe we can invite him to church with us. Everyone's for that, aren't they?"

"Yes, of course," Mrs. O'Connor said. "But I'm still not sure about letting you go over to his house."

"We'll just be down the street," Ally reassured her mom. "And I promise I'll get Jeff's aunt to come by and meet you. Or better yet, invite you over to her house."

"Just don't let him pull anything on you," Mr. O'Connor said. "We'll meet his aunt in due time."

"The sooner the better," Mrs. O'Connor added. "Before you go, Ally, the dishes. Nick, Molly, help her."

"Oh, man, I thought I was a guest," Nick said.

"You, sir, are no guest," Mrs. O'Connor said, smiling. "You practically live here. So clean up. You too, Molly."

Nick sighed, and Ally smiled at him. "Come on. I'll show you how to really clean off a table right. I'll clean, Nick. You put the dishes in the dishwasher. Molly can clear the table."

"Aye, aye, sir," Molly said.

But Nick just stood there. "Come on, Nick," Ally prodded. "You know what to do."

"Naturally, I get the crummy jobs," Nick said morosely.

❧

22

A half an hour later, they stood in front of the door of Jeff's house. It wasn't one of the biggest houses in the development, but it looked neat, with a well-manicured garden and a green lawn. Ally used the knocker.

"Are you sure about this?" Nick said as they waited.

"Jeff's harmless," Ally replied.

"What about his aunt? Maybe she's really a zombie."

"Oh, come on," Molly said. "I'm sure everyone is normal here."

At that moment, the door opened, and a tall, smiling woman answered. Her face almost glowed from her questioning smile. She was attractive, though her nose was a bit on the large side.

"Yes?" she said.

"Is this where Jeff Reynolds lives?"

Before the lady could answer, Jeff appeared behind her. "Hey, Ally, you came." He eyed Nick and Molly, smiling.

The lady said to Jeff, "These are your friends?"

"Yeah, we're going to play some poker."

"Poker?" Ally and Nick exclaimed at the same time.

Jeff's aunt looked exasperated. "Uh, Jeff, we talked about that, didn't we?"

"Just kidding," Jeff said with a slight scowl. "Sheesh. Monopoly, anyone?"

Jeff's aunt held out a bony but firm hand. "Since Jeff has obviously forgotten his manners, I'll introduce myself. I'm Jeff's aunt, Barbara. Most people call me Babs. My last name is Kruck."

Ally took her hand and pressed it. Miss Kruck's shake was firm and dry. "Pleased to meet you, Miss Kruck. I'm Ally O'Connor, and this is Nick Parker and his sister, Molly."

Miss Kruck then shook hands with Nick and Molly. "Okay, these are the rules," she said after the introductions. Jeff sighed heavily behind her, but when she turned to him and said, "Now that'll be enough of that," he shrugged. "Jeff has to get his beauty sleep. So please, no later than

9:30. Otherwise, the house is yours. The fridge has some nice lunch meat in it."

"Oh, we just ate awhile ago," Ally said.

"If I know kids," Miss Kruck said, "at about 8:30 you'll want another feast. So feel free. Now Jeff, show them around the house, and then you can all play in the family room. I'll disappear for the duration."

"Thanks, Aunt Barbara," Jeff said.

The house was musty, with old, ornate couches in the living room, tall, shining wooden tables and hutches in the dining room, and a cozy setup in the family room with rich, red leather chairs around a tea table.

When Miss Kruck was gone, Jeff said, "Don't worry about my Aunt Barbara. She won't bother us."

"She's very nice," Ally said.

"Soft on the outside. Hard on the inside." Jeff said dryly.

Ally wondered about that comment, but didn't respond.

Nick broke the uncomfortable silence. "She kind of reminds me—"

"Of the witch in *The Wizard of Oz*?" Jeff interrupted.

Ally couldn't stand it anymore. "Good grief," she said, shooting Nick a disapproving look, then turning to Jeff. "You don't think much of your aunt, do you? She seems really nice to me."

"Just get to know her is all I ask," Jeff said. "Or better yet . . . don't."

Ally wanted to change the subject. She didn't like Jeff speaking disrespectfully about an adult, especially one who seemed, for all purposes, decent and kind.

Nick met Ally's glance knowingly. Miss Kruck had given them the whole house and said they could have anything in the refrigerator. His look seemed to say: *What more can you ask for from an adult?*

The thought made her smile, and Jeff said, "What are you grinning about?"

"Nothing," Ally said. "I like your house. It's—"

"Old," Jeff said.

"Classy, I was going to say," Ally answered, annoyed with Jeff's habit of interrupting and adding nothing but negative comments to the conversation.

"If you say so." Jeff led them into the family room, and they all took a seat. Shelves filled with books lined the walls, set off by rich, old leather couches, a love seat, and an easy chair. Ally noticed that many of the books were by Christian personalities she recognized—Billy Graham, Max Lucado, and others.

Jeff pulled the Monopoly game out from under the couch. "Which do you want?" he asked everyone. "The dog, the car, or—"

This time Nick interrupted. "I'll be the car."

"I'll be the dog," piped up Molly.

"I'll be the little hat," Ally said.

"Ah yes, a true fashion plate," Jeff said.

Ally glanced at Nick and saw his eyes fixed on Jeff's face with a mixture of jealousy and disgust. "Well, I am a princess," she said. "So says my mother, anyway."

"Yes, milady," Jeff said. "And I will be happy to beat you in the game of Monopoly."

"Go ahead and try."

They started the game, and Jeff kept the conversation going about Mrs. Hanson's horses and the farm and numerous other things. When Ally could get in a word edgewise, she asked, "Do you know about the houses down the street being broken into?"

"Yeah," Jeff said. "I heard about it. Probably some bad kid." He grinned.

What does he mean by that? Ally wondered, but pressed on. "Well, if it is, I hope they catch him before he hits our house."

"Or her," Nick said.

"Her?" Ally looked puzzled.

"It *could* be a her," Nick said.

"Yeah, right." Ally rolled her eyes in Molly's direction.

"Hey," Molly said, teasing, "I could be a burglar."

"Yeah, right, an eleven-year-old burglar," Nick scoffed.

Jeff rolled the dice. "It's probably someone in the neighborhood," he said. "A neighbor would be in the best position to know when other neighbors are gone."

Ally looked at Jeff with interest and respect. "That's a keen insight."

"Right, that's me, the master of keen insights. Rats, I just landed on your property."

"Pay up, buddy," Ally said, laughing. She flipped through her wad of Monopoly money, remembering how Jeff had known where her house was. "By the way, speaking of knowing the neighborhood, how did you know where I lived?"

"Good guess. It looked like you. Slim. Beautiful. Colorful."

"Thanks for the compliments, but I don't buy it."

"I've seen you guys around," he said. "We go that way when Aunt Barbara takes me to town with her. You spend a lot of time on the lawn."

"Football," Nick said, eager to get a word in.

"Yeah, I've seen you throwing around one."

Ally mulled this over. It seemed odd that Jeff would know where she lived, but she decided to forget it. Jeff was probably just curious, like her, to snoop out things like that.

When the game was over and everyone had eaten a ham sandwich and finished a can of Coke, Miss Kruck appeared with a book in her hand. Ally noticed it was *Christy,* a novel by Catherine Marshall, one of her favorites.

"Oh, you're reading *Christy*?" Ally said.

"She reads it once a year," Jeff said in a bored tone.

"It's a wonderful book, Jeff," Miss Kruck said, then turned to Ally. "I've been trying to get him to read it, but you know boys."

"It's one of my all-time favorites," Ally said. "Molly's too."

Molly nodded enthusiastically.

"Mine too," Miss Kruck said. "You'll have to come over and talk books with me some time. You too, Molly. But meanwhile, I think it's time you kids headed off for home, don't you think, Jeff?"

Jeff blew frustrated air out of his mouth.

"Now, come on," Miss Kruck said. "You know the rules."

"Okay, guys," Jeff said, giving his aunt a glare, "guess it's time to go. I had a good time. Thanks for coming over."

Miss Kruck and Jeff walked with Nick, Molly, and Ally out to the front door.

"Can we hang out again tomorrow?" Jeff asked.

Ally realized he must be very lonely to latch on to her and the Parkers so quickly. "Sure," she said, noting Nick's disapproving look.

"Okay, I'll see you then."

"Really, do come by for a book talk," Miss Kruck added as the kids filed out the door.

Ally's eyes lit up. "I'd like that."

"Me too," Molly chimed in.

On the way home, Nick tugged at Ally to hang back from Molly for a minute. He looked serious. "This is getting weird, Ally."

"Why do you say that?"

"The guy obviously has a crush on you."

"So what? I'm not allowed to date till I'm sixteen—and you know that. Can't Jeff and I just be friends?"

"I thought we were friends."

"We are."

"Well, I think Jeff's going to get in the way."

Ally gave Nick a playful shove and caught up with Molly. "Come on, he's just a lonely guy. I'm not interested in him that way anyway."

"Then how are you interested in him?"

"As a friend."

"Plus, his aunt's really nice," Molly said. "I already like her better than Jeff. What's with him anyway? Why is he so mean to her?"

Ally shook her head. "I don't know. I get the idea Jeff would rather live somewhere else."

"With his dad, maybe?" Molly asked.

"I don't know," Ally said, then muttered to herself, "But I'd like to find out."

Nick sighed heavily as they reached Ally's house. "Okay, I'll be friends with him. But don't expect me to like him."

Ally laughed. "Sometimes, you don't make much sense, Nick. See you tomorrow."

"Yeah."

Ally turned to Molly. "Are you staying over, Moll?"

"Yeah, I brought my sleeping bag."

"Great," Ally said. "We can sit up and sip geranium tea and talk about Nick and Jeff."

"Ha, ha," Nick said as he backed away.

Ally and Molly watched Nick head off into the darkness. Ally grinned. Boys were so crazy sometimes.

"Come on, Molly. Let's get to bed."

Four

Visitors

Molly and Ally lay on the beds in Ally's room. Molly had her sleeping bag on top of the covers so she wouldn't have to make the bed in the morning. Mrs. O'Connor always made Ally make her bed neatly.

The girls talked till past 11:00, but gradually they tired and began to settle down toward sleep. As Ally closed her eyes and listened to the night noises of crickets and frogs, she heard a tapping on her window.

She popped up in bed. Her eyes were adjusted to the darkness, but she couldn't make out what was doing the tapping.

"What's that noise?" Molly whispered.

Ally got up and walked over to the window. A strange, almost hideous figure was right up against the pane. It was Jeff. He had his lips and nose pressed up against the window pane, his teeth bared like a werewolf.

"It's Jeff!" Ally said, turning to Molly, who had gotten out of bed.

"Just ignore him," Molly said.

But Ally thrust open the window. "Jeff! What on earth are you doing here?"

"I just wanted a kiss goodnight."

"Well, you're not getting one. Go to bed."

"Here? In the pricker bushes?"

Molly giggled. "Go home, you goofball!"

Jeff grinned. "I'm always home. Home is where the heart is."

"You're nuts. I think you really better go home, Jeff," Ally said.

"Okay, okay. Good night, ladies. See you on the morrow. I shall return to my dungeon and meal of cold gruel."

Ally and Molly stood at the window, watching as Jeff trudged away. Then Molly crawled back into her sleeping bag, saying, "I'm beginning to think he *is* a nutcase."

"Maybe." Ally slid between the sheets of her bed, smiling in the dark. "I can't believe he likes me."

"Why not? You're a funny person."

"Oh, come on."

"You are, Ally. But I think Nick is right. You'd better watch out. This guy is a little weird."

"I'll have a private investigator check him out tomorrow."

Molly giggled. "See? You are a funny person!"

The next morning, the O'Connors ate breakfast at about 8:30. Ally's dad worked as a manager of a machinery company in town; he usually left at about 8:45. Since it was still summer, August, Ally didn't have to get up early for school.

"I guess we'll be going by to see Ally's one true love then," Molly said as she munched on a piece of toast.

Ally's parents said "What!" at the same time.

Molly grinned and stuffed the rest of the toast in her mouth.

Mrs. O'Connor looked at Ally. "Well?"

"He's fourteen years old, Mom. And I know I can't date till I'm sixteen."

"Some kids do it on the sly," Mrs. O'Connor said. "I'm not going to tolerate you sneaking off with this boy unchaperoned—"

"I'm not sneaking off anywhere," Ally interrupted, then paused. *How did I pick up Jeff's bad habit of interrupting people?* Seeing her father's expectant look, she continued. "Nick or Molly will always be there with us."

"Well, I should hope so," Mr. O'Connor said. "But I'd feel better if I knew who this boy was."

"Look," Ally said, giving Molly a hard look, hoping she wouldn't say anything about last night's window episode, "he's just kind of attached himself to us. I guess he's lonely. But I don't hardly know who he is, except that he lives with a nice lady who reads *Christy* every year and is a committed Christian."

"She is?" Mrs. O'Connor said.

"Yeah," Molly said. "She's really kind of cool."

"But how do you know she's a Christian, honey?" Mrs. O'Connor said to Ally.

"Jeff told me. Apparently, he doesn't like her talking about Jesus with him."

"So he's not . . . a Christian?"

"I guess not."

Mrs. O'Connor said to her husband, "We ought to have them over for dinner."

"All right by me," Mr. O'Connor said, getting up and brushing crumbs off his tie. "I've got to run."

"Kiss," Mrs. O'Connor said.

Mr. O'Connor kissed his wife, then rolled his eyes at Molly and Ally. Ally did like it that her parents loved each other. She knew that wasn't the way it was for a lot of

31

kids, and she appreciated the little things they did to show affection. But sometimes, like now, it embarrassed her in front of Molly. Ally instinctively began cleaning up.

Behind them, there was a knock at the door.

"Hey," Nick said, walking in. "Everybody fed and waked up?"

"Hi, Nick," Mrs. O'Connor said. "I expect you to be the chaperone around this new boy, you understand."

"Sure," Nick said, walking over to the table and snagging a leftover piece of toast. "I'll make him dance to my tune. I'll put him in chains if he gets out of line. I'll—"

"Okay, okay," Mrs. O'Connor said. "I think just being there should be enough."

Nick grinned at Ally, who placed a pile of dishes in the sink.

A second later, there was another knock.

"What is this, Grand Central Station?" Mrs. O'Connor said, laughing.

Nick opened the door and stepped back, making a motion with his hand. "Lord Jeff of the vale," he announced.

Jeff walked in and Ally noticed her mother giving him a careful look.

"So you're Jeff?"

Jeff held out his hand. "Yeah. Is that bad?"

Mrs. O'Connor took it and stared into Jeff's eyes. "All I care is that there's no funny business with these kids. Do you understand?"

"Yes, ma'am," Jeff said.

"Good." Mrs. O'Connor turned to Ally. "I suppose you all are traipsing off somewhere?"

"Not me," Molly said. "I have to go home and do some chores."

"We'll be around, Mom," Ally said.

"Actually," Jeff interjected, "I'd like to take whoever wants to go to meet a friend of mine."

"Who might that be?" Mrs. O'Connor said.

"He lives back in the woods behind the houses. He's really a neat guy, and I thought, well, I thought Ally and Nick might like to meet him. Since they seem to think I'm so mysterious and all."

"I don't know about this," Mrs. O'Connor said with uncertainty.

"He's just a regular guy," Jeff said. "Doesn't do anything bad. He's the most natural guy I know. I promise, he's really nice."

"Well, all right. Just so you're back at lunchtime," Mrs. O'Connor said to Ally.

Molly left and Ally and Nick finished cleaning up. Then they walked up the road with Jeff toward the covered bridge.

"Your mom is nice," Jeff said.

Ally laughed. "She slings around orders sometimes, but I love her."

"Yeah," Jeff said. "I wish I had a mom like that."

No one said anything, and the only sound was their running shoes padding on the pavement.

"What happened to your mom, anyway?" Nick said, breaking the silence.

"She had breast cancer."

"I'm so sorry," Ally said.

"It's okay," Jeff replied. "It was when I was little. I didn't even know her."

"So you've been living with your aunt since then?" Nick asked.

They walked through the covered bridge, keeping to the right side of the road.

"Pretty much," Jeff said. "Except when I lived with my dad."

"So how come you don't live with him now?"

Jeff suddenly took off running on the other side of the covered bridge. He raced down a trail into the trees.

"Guess we'll have to ask that question later," Nick said and plunged into the woods after Jeff.

Ally hurried after both of them.

Five

The Man in the Woods

Jeff sprinted ahead of them through the deep woods. Ally hadn't realized how thick the trees were here; she'd never really explored them. It had never occurred to her that someone might live in the woods, almost secluded from the rest of civilization.

She caught Nick just as they both reached the top of a hill. Jeff stood there in the morning light, panting. He stared down at something, and Ally followed his line of sight.

There, in a small valley between hills, stood a cabin with smoke drifting lazily from the chimney.

"What is it?"

"Coombsie," Jeff said.

"Coombs who?" Nick asked.

"Come on, I'll introduce you."

The three of them tramped down to the valley and reached the rustic, rusty-hinged door. Jeff knocked.

A man with a gray beard answered within seconds. He had twinkly green eyes and was wearing clothes made out of deerskin. "Hey," he said smiling, his teeth clenching a pipe.

"Coombsie," Jeff exclaimed. "These are my new friends. Ally and Nick. They're riding horses over at Mrs. Hanson's." Jeff grabbed the man's arm. "This," he announced, "is my friend, Nestor Coombs. Everyone calls him Coombsie."

"Come on in," Coombsie said and motioned for them to enter.

The cabin was one room that had a fire burning in the fireplace. All around the walls hung the stuffed heads of various animals—a bear, a couple of deer, birds, even two gray squirrels. Ally didn't care for the animals, but she did think the cabin quaint.

Coombsie sat in an old armchair, and Jeff took a seat on a bench made out of a split log. Jeff patted the wood. "This is where you guys sit. Coombsie's place isn't laid out like my aunt's. No leather furniture."

"But that doesn't mean I won't have it someday," Coombsie said. "When the government sends me the money they owe me."

"Coombsie's always talking about the government owing him money," Jeff said. "It's a joke. Laugh."

Ally smiled and Nick stared around the room, then they both plunked down on the split log.

"So you bagged anything lately?" Jeff said.

"Got a buck the other day. Been eatin' good," Coombsie replied. He gestured to the fireplace, where a large pot hung over the fire. Ally sniffed the gamey aroma of cooking venison. "Carcass is hanging out back," Coombsie said matter-of-factly. Ally decided she wouldn't take a look if she could help it. When it came to hunting deer, she definitely sided with Bambi.

"So, have you eaten any more little kids lately?" Jeff asked Coombsie.

"Just had one for breakfast. Nice little boy," Coombsie answered, blowing smoke rings out of his circled lips.

Jeff laughed, but Ally didn't. Coombsie looked enough like a wild man for her to believe that anything might be possible with him.

Jeff sensed Ally's uncertainty. "Coombsie and I joke like this all the time," he assured her. "He wouldn't harm a flea, except for the animals he kills to eat, that is."

Ally just smiled at Coombsie and nodded her head.

Coombsie smiled back, then leaned forward. "So, what's the news?" he said to Jeff.

"Haven't heard from him," Jeff replied mysteriously.

"What are you going to do?"

"I was thinking of coming and living with you," Jeff said.

Coombsie took the pipe out of his mouth. "I'd love to have you. You know that. But I don't think it would be a good idea."

"Yeah, I guess. I'd just mess up your life, anyway."

"What are you talking about?" Ally interjected. "Who haven't you heard from?"

"My father."

Coombsie suddenly stood, rapping on the arm of the chair.

Ally sat very still, wondering what was going on.

"Oh, come on," Jeff said to Coombsie.

Coombsie knocked again.

"What is it?" Ally said, suddenly feeling a little frightened.

"It's a knock-knock joke," Jeff said. "Can't you tell?"

Coombsie shook his head and knocked again.

Jeff whispered with mock seriousness, "This is why Coombsie isn't married. He has limited entertainment interests. Just play along, okay?"

Ally glanced at Nick as Coombsie knocked again.

"Who's there?" Ally said cautiously.

"Ally," Coombsie said.

"Ally who?"

"That's what I want to know," Coombsie said and sat down.

Jeff laughed. "Sorry! Her last name is O'Connor. And Nick's is Parker." He turned to Ally. "Coombsie likes to use knock knock-jokes to ask questions sometimes."

"Really?" Ally said.

"Yeah, it's his way of getting someone's attention when he's not sure they're paying attention."

Coombsie knocked again and Jeff said, "Who's there?"

"Jeff," Coombsie said.

"Jeff who?"

"Jeff, what will you do?"

Ally thought she understood and said, "Where is your father, Jeff?"

"Hiding."

"What do you mean, hiding?"

"He's . . . I don't know."

There was an awkward silence, then Coombsie knocked again.

"Who's there?" Nick said this time.

"You want . . ."

"You want what?" Nick said, grinning at Ally.

"You want to hear my latest story?"

Jeff clapped his hands together like an excited four-year-old in Sunday school. "All right!" To Nick and Ally he said, "Coombsie writes stories."

Coombsie put his finger to his head and leaned back as if meditating. Suddenly, he shot forward, his face animated, alive, almost glowing with excitement.

"All the fair feathered friends were imprisoned," Coombsie said. "The cruel prince had captured them, put them in cages. But lo! There was enchantment in the land, and the two great ones came over the mountain to work it. Just the two of them. In search of their destiny. In search of hope.

"They were young—they hadn't aged in centuries. They only wanted rest and hope and peace. And to set their friends free."

38

Jeff whispered, "All his great characters want peace and hope."

Coombsie put his finger to his lips. "Shhhhh! You can hear them if you listen. On the wind. Their voices like pine trees in a breeze, their eyes sad and gray but hopeful. They come with their heads back, and they smile into the river, and they know they will find what they're looking for there. His name is Jason the Unblemished. Hers, Marianne the Matchless. They go into the stream. They look down. Diamonds. Rubies. Emeralds. They dip down deep. They grasp the jewels and hold them up to the sun. The jewels sparkle. Then . . ."

Jeff grinned. "This is the good part."

"They take a bite. The emerald tastes like all the great cities of the world in their glory. The diamonds taste of an artist's tears after he has finished his greatest work. The ruby—the ruby is the best; it tastes of fair earth and blessed heaven and all the joys of creation. And then . . ."

Jeff whispered, "Watch this."

Coombsie waved his hands upward. "The transformation comes. They both become . . . they become completely . . . they become all they were meant to be."

Jeff sat as though transfixed while Coombsie put his finger to his lips again. "They're able to mount the sky, to seek the farthest horizon, to filch the gold at the end of the rainbow. They are transformed. Friends who can help friends must look like them. They're sparrows!"

"Sparrows!" Ally almost shouted, caught up in the story.

Again, the finger to the lips. "They fly off to the castle, where the cruel prince has imprisoned all the fair feathered friends. The sparrows fly in. They beat their wings at the prince. They flail. They screech. They bring him to his knees, and he cries out, 'What do you want?' They say, 'Set our friends free.' And the prince, cowering and terrified, obliges. He opens every cage. And every fair feathered friend emerges, singing his song and flying into the heavens."

39

Coombsie paused and then clapped his hands. "Ha!"

Jeff banged his hands on his knees. "Cool!" To Ally and Nick he said, "Coombsie's stories always involve setting things free."

"That was really interesting, Mr. Coombs," Ally said.

"Yeah, cool," Nick added. "But what happened to Jason and Marianne?"

Coombsie nodded. "They ate once again of the rubies, emeralds, and diamonds, then transformed back. And the ruby hardened, so they sold it and went to the Great City, where every video game that's ever been invented is free. And they played and played and played. And won too."

"Whoa," Jeff said.

Coombsie knocked on the chair arms again, his face full of delight.

"Who's there?"

"Now some . . ." Coombsie said.

"Now some who?" Jeff asked, his face aglow like Coombsie's.

"Now some music."

Jeff turned to Nick and Ally. "Prepare to be amazed."

Six

Music Extraordinaire

Coombsie grabbed a violin out of an ancient case, put it to his neck, and began to play. At first the sounds were scratchy, meaningless, but soon he captured a tune. He played skillfully, beautifully, heart-wrenchingly.

Ally was soon caught up in the mournful yet powerful tones of the music. Coombsie looked transported, his eyes closed, also caught up in the music. He went up and down the neck of the violin like a master, bringing together the melodies of rock tunes Ally recognized and linking them— no, spinning them—into a wondrous melody that had everyone in the room enraptured.

Coombsie's fingers roved the violin like he'd played it every day since birth. Ally had heard some of the greatest violinists in the world—her parents believed strongly in exposing her to great music—and she thought that Coombsie sounded as good as any of them.

Jeff whispered to Ally as Coombsie played renditions of songs from the Beatles, the Beach Boys, and other old bands Ally's mother and father often listened to. "Coombsie's been playing the violin since he was a little kid."

The music was more compelling than anything Ally had ever heard. She almost felt as if she couldn't listen anymore for the joy and pain that resounded in the simplest parts of the melody.

Then, suddenly, the spell was broken. Coombsie's eyes popped open.

"They've come again!"

Jeff jumped up. "No. NO!"

Coombsie threw the violin onto the bed. He grabbed a bullhorn off a table in the corner and ran to the door. Jeff tried to stop him, grabbing him by the shoulders.

"You have to conquer it, Coombsie!"

"They've come back!" Coombsie yelled, his face twisted in anguish. He looked terrified. He pushed past Jeff to the door, threw it open, and put the bullhorn to his lips.

"Go away!" he cried. "Go away. I won't listen to you." He stuck his free hand over an ear and exploded into the horn, "I won't listen to you!"

Jeff tried to pull Coombsie back into the room, but Coombsie threw him off and ran out into the clearing in front of the cabin.

"I'll make you go away," he shouted into the bullhorn. "I'll never listen to you."

Jeff looked at Nick and Ally, who were staring out the window at Coombsie. "I'm sorry about this," he said. "I didn't think it would happen today. I'm really sorry. It only happens once in awhile, but when it does . . ."

"What is it?" Ally said, listening to Coombsie roar into the bullhorn like a maniac.

"Come on," Jeff said, his eyes dark. "Maybe you can help."

They all walked out the door. Coombsie had dropped the bullhorn from his mouth and was standing over something on the ground, looking down at it. When Jeff cautiously touched his shoulder, he looked up with tears in his eyes.

"I drove them away."

Ally started to speak, but Jeff motioned for her to be quiet. Coombsie just stood there, the bullhorn still dangling from his hand.

"Which one was it, Coombsie?" Jeff finally said.

"All of them."

"The bad ones?"

"Yeah."

Ally wasn't sure what was going on. Jeff took her and Nick both aside.

"Look," he said. "I don't expect you to get this, but Coombsie sees ghosts. He was in Vietnam, and the ghosts of Vietcong soldiers he killed haunt him. He came here to get away from them. But he thinks the ghosts have found him. He can hear them laughing, and when he does, he tries to scare them away. That's what he thinks, anyway."

"What can we do?" Ally said, her voice catching in her throat.

"I want to help him, Ally. That's all. He's my friend."

Ally and Nick glanced at one another uneasily. Ally spoke up.

"Coombsie?"

"Yeah?"

"Do you ever talk to them?"

"They don't talk. They just laugh," Coombsie said wearily. He slipped to his knees, dropping the bullhorn.

"What's he doing now?" Ally whispered.

"Just be quiet," Jeff whispered back.

Coombsie's voice was low, barely audible. Small, almost squealing noises came from his mouth; he almost sounded like an animal in pain. His head was bowed. He was praying. Ally prayed too, desperate for God to give her some insight into how to help Coombsie.

Coombsie's voice rose, and he beat his chest with a fist. "Please stop me from seeing them! Please! Stop them and make me whole again." Then he slowly rose, picked up the bullhorn, and walked slowly, sadly, toward the cabin. Jeff followed him, with Nick and Ally close behind.

When they entered the cabin, Jeff put his hand on Coombsie's shoulder. "It's okay," he said. "It'll be okay this time."

"It'll never be okay," Coombsie replied as he put the bullhorn back on the table and sat on a chair, looking glum and tired. "They come back. They always come back."

Jeff kept his hand on Coombsie's shoulder. "I just know it'll be okay someday, Coombsie. I just know it."

"Yeah," Coombsie said without any conviction. It was as if the life had suddenly drained out of him.

Jeff looked sadly at Nick and Ally. "We'd better go. He needs to be alone now."

Ally nodded, then stopped in front of Coombsie. She said, "I loved your story and the music, Mr. Coombs. I'd like to pray for you. Can I pray for you?"

Coombsie looked up at her as if seeing her for the first time. He blinked and then turned away.

"There's nothing anyone can do," he said and stared into his hands.

Jeff grabbed Ally's hand and pulled her away. They walked slowly to the door and stepped out into the late morning sunlight.

The three of them trudged through the woods for awhile before Nick finally broke the silence.

"I really feel bad for him."

"Yeah," Jeff said.

Ally glanced at him. "Are you okay, Jeff?"

"Yeah."

"Maybe he should see a doctor."

"He's been through that," Jeff said. "He's been through everything. This is the closest he's ever come, I think. Usually, it's worse."

"What has he come close to?" Nick asked.

"What he wants."

"What is that?"

The trail ended, and they stepped out onto a back road. "To be whole again. He doesn't usually pray."

They walked along in silence. Only their shoes made noise as they scuffled on the dirt.

Jeff said suddenly, "Look, I'm sorry. I didn't know it would happen again."

Ally touched his shoulder. "Jeff, it's okay. I like Coombsie. He's really unique. But I don't know how to help him, except to pray."

"Yeah, and we all know what praying does."

"What's that supposed to mean?"

"Nothing. Don't worry about it. Look, you want to go to the Hanson's and ride for awhile? I think I need to do something that will take my mind off this."

"Good idea."

"It would be a relief," Nick said.

They came around a corner and reached the main road down to the farm.

Going for a Ride

The three walked up the road and reached Mrs. Hanson's house in a few minutes. In another ten minutes they were all saddled up, ready for a cattle drive. Ally rode Snowbird, Nick had Lucky, and Jeff took the majestic Thunder.

Before they left, Mrs. Hanson said, "Don't take Thunder by that burned-out farm, Jeff."

"Oh, how come?"

"He likes their little pond. Just plunges in. Last time he got stuck, and we had to pull him out."

"Wow. We were just there a couple of days ago."

Ally laughed. "He just wants to cool off."

"Right, but I wasn't at all cooled off when we were done getting him out," Mrs. Hanson said with a grin. "Just keep Thunder reined in tight. He's been rather frisky the last few days."

"Right," Jeff said, glancing at Nick and Ally.

They all trotted off down the road, heading in the opposite direction from the Matthews' farm. As they plodded along, Ally said, "You're not going to take us to another mountain man's cabin, are you, Jeff?"

"Nope. Let's roll."

Jeff kicked Thunder, and soon they were all cantering along the road, evergreens and thick leaves brushing at them. When they slowed back down to a walk, Ally said, "How do you know all these people, Jeff?"

"Oh, I get around."

Ally was silent for a moment, then said, "Jeff, I've been meaning to ask you: What *do* you know about thieves breaking into houses in our neighborhood?"

"Just that they never steal much."

"They don't?"

"Mostly electronic stuff, I think. They seem to mainly like tearing the houses up."

"You don't think Coombsie'd be doing it, do you? He could have a lot of anger, I think."

"Nah. Anyway, he's rich. Why would he want to steal?"

"He's rich?"

"He gets all kinds of special checks from the government, because of his disabilities and wounds from combat."

"I don't think that's rich."

"It is in my book. Come on. Let's ride."

Jeff took off again. Ally looked at Nick and said, "He certainly likes to go all the time, doesn't he?"

"Hey, he's a young guy with spirit," Nick said. "Except it isn't the Holy Spirit, I don't think."

"I was going to talk to him about that. Why don't you jump in sometimes?"

Nick just shrugged. Ally looked away from him and gazed down the road where Jeff had just whizzed around a corner.

"Well, I guess we better ride."

"Yeah."

They stormed up the road, caught Jeff, and then galloped along, cheering and razzing one another. Suddenly, a bunch of dogs ripped out of the woods ahead of them. Jeff pulled up short, as did Ally and Nick.

"What are they?" Nick asked.

"Dump dogs from the landfill down the road," Jeff said. "Let's not tango with them."

"What will they do?" Ally asked nervously.

"Chase the horses. They're a bit on the wild side," Jeff turned around Thunder and began loping back in the direction they'd come. Ally wheeled and followed, with Nick close behind her. The dogs began barking and pursuing.

"Go!" Jeff yelled.

All three of them kicked their horses into a full gallop, and the dogs were soon left in the dust. When the dogs were well out of sight, Jeff slowed down to a walk. Ally came up next to him, with Nick on her left.

"Where do the dogs come from?" she asked.

"People get rid of them, let them off in the woods," Jeff said. "Some run away. Some are born to be wild."

"Poor things," Ally said. "They should be in a shelter."

"And put to sleep?" Jeff asked. "I don't think they'd want that."

They rode for a while longer and soon were in sight of the Hanson farmhouse.

"Well, that was a good ride," Jeff said. "Thanks for coming. Guess we can clean up and be on our way."

After the horseback riding, the threesome returned to the stables, brushed down the horses, and headed for home.

As they approached Jeff's house, he stopped. "Guess I'll see you later."

"Yeah, see you later," Ally said.

"Thanks for letting us meet Coombsie, Jeff," Nick said, surprising Ally. "I hope he starts to feel better."

"Yeah, well, you know how these things go. Anyway, I'll see you later."

"Be good," Ally said and started for her house. Nick walked beside her, not saying much.

48

"You want some lunch?" Ally said when they got to her house.

"You really like him, don't you?" Nick asked, ignoring her question.

"He's okay. I like the horseback riding. I like meeting new people. I don't know about Jeff."

"What do you mean?"

"I think we should talk to my mom about him."

"Yeah, maybe we should."

Eight

The Carnival Contest

When they stepped into the kitchen, Mrs. O'Connor looked up from preparing lunch. "Have a good time?"

"Yeah, we met an interesting man, that friend of Jeff's."

"We rode the horses again too," Nick said, opening the refrigerator and pulling out a Coke. "I'm beginning to feel like Roy Rogers."

"Those horses will make you bowlegged," Mrs. O'Connor said, opening a can.

"What're you making, Mom?" Ally asked.

"Grilled cheese sandwiches and tomato soup."

"Mmm, good."

"Your favorite."

"Right." Ally glanced at Nick, then turned back to her mom. "Look, I want to ask you something."

"Shoot."

"Were some of the soldiers who were in Vietnam really messed up by it?" She and Nick sat down at the table.

"A lot of people were messed up by Vietnam, honey. Agent Orange. Killing innocent people. Atrocities. There was a lot of bad stuff going on back then."

50

"This friend of Jeff's," Nick said. "He was in Vietnam. Apparently, he killed a lot of people and was wounded and everything. But he thinks he sees ghosts."

"How old would people be today who were in Vietnam?" Ally added.

Mrs. O'Connor turned from the stove, a worried look on her face. "Late forties, I guess," she said. "Same age as me and your dad. Your dad almost got drafted, but he was in college when President Nixon sponsored the draft lottery, and he got a high number."

"What was the draft lottery?" Nick asked.

"Everyone's birth date got put in a pot. They pulled them out one by one. The first one hundred or so had a good chance of being drafted. The others didn't have to worry."

"So it was a way to do what?" Ally asked.

"Make it more fair," Mrs. O'Connor said, flipping over a sandwich on the stove. "A lot of the draftees in those days were young men who didn't go to college—didn't have the money. Blue-collar type people. A lot of politicians thought it was unfair that young men who went to college got out of the draft for the four years they were in college. So it was Nixon's way of making it more fair."

"So Dad got a high number?" Ally said.

"Yes, in the high two hundreds, I think. We celebrated that one. The war got a lot worse after that, even though Nixon said we were pulling out."

"Worse?" Nick asked.

"My Lai had happened before we pulled out, for one thing," Mrs. O'Connor answered as she set the sandwiches and soup in front of them. "That was what a lot of the protesting was about. A Lieutenant Calley and his men killed a bunch of civilians—regular folks, not soldiers—at a village called My Lai in Vietnam. It was all over the news. A real atrocity. A lot of soldiers who came back from Vietnam said that was just one of many. But I suppose it was hard for them too. In Vietnam, you never knew who was the enemy and who was on your side." Mrs. O'Connor shook her head. "It was an awful war."

"All war is awful, isn't it?" Ally whispered to herself, then louder said, "I wonder if Coombsie saw those kinds of things."

"If he was there for long," Mrs. O'Connor said. "If he was a frontline grunt, as they called them, he probably saw enough."

"I wonder if he was involved in any of it," Ally answered, then took the last bite of her sandwich, sending it down with a gulp of ice water.

"This man isn't doing anything dangerous, is he?" Mrs. O'Connor suddenly asked.

"No. He seems nice enough. He just sees these ghosts and yells at them through a bullhorn."

"He yells at them through a bullhorn?"

"Mom," Ally said, "it's not that bad. He's harmless, I think."

"Well, be careful. Don't visit him alone."

"I know, Mom." She turned to Nick. "Well, school is next week. Want to do anything cool before we have to get back to the grind?"

"Go outside and let it happen as it happens," Nick said. "But I wouldn't mind doing some roller-blading."

"Hey, that sounds like fun. Let's do it."

"Don't go too far," Mrs. O'Connor said. "I need you to do some chores later, Ally."

"Okay."

Ally retrieved her roller-blades from under her bed, then she and Nick walked to Nick's house to get his.

Ally and Nick strapped on their roller-blades and began skating in the street.

"Let's go up and see if Jeff wants to do it too," Ally said.

Nick frowned but followed her, and soon they stood at Jeff's house. Ally walked up the steps and knocked. Miss Kruck answered.

"Oh, Jeff would like that. He's really good at it," she said when Ally asked about roller-blading. Miss Kruck called Jeff, and he came out, looking a little rumpled.

"I was taking a nap," he explained.

"We were just doing some roller-blading. Thought you might want to come."

"Yeah, okay. Give me two minutes."

Jeff returned a few minutes later, looking spiffed up and ready to roll.

Soon they were zooming up the street, Jeff in the lead going backwards and forwards and even performing a cart-wheel.

"You're amazing," Ally said when she caught her breath.

"Thanks. You're not so bad yourself. Hey, we ought to do the Labor Day carnival," Jeff said.

Ally knew about the carnival their town featured every year on Labor Day weekend, but she didn't know what Jeff was referring to. "What do you mean?"

"The talent show," Jeff said. "My aunt told me about it. People do all kinds of things, but I have a horse costume and a knight costume. Two people do the horse and one the knight. It's hilarious."

"Cool. You want to try it, Nick?" Ally asked.

"Okay with me," Nick answered.

"I'll get it right now. We'll have to practice big time to get ready. Let's go back to the house. We can practice in the big circle there." Jeff's house was on a cul-de-sac, which terminated in a circle large enough for a roller rink.

Jeff took Nick and Ally down into his basement, where he found a large box. He pulled out the costumes and showed them to the twosome.

"Everything's here," Jeff said. "You and Nick could be the horse, and I'll be the knight."

They walked back out into the sunshine. Ally saw that the circle of the cul-de-sac was perfect for skating.

"What do we do?" Ally asked.

"It's simple," Jeff said. He laid the costume out, then showed them how to get into it. Ally took the rear position, with Nick in the head. When the horse costume was draped over them, Jeff said, "Practice skating around so you get used to the position."

At first, they kept bumping into each other, but in a matter of minutes, they were able to skate freely.

Then Jeff donned the helmet and colors. "Okay, now the knight comes out to get his horse, and the horse tries to get away. He keeps trying to mount the horse, but keeps falling. It's really funny, if you get into it."

"Let's try it," Ally said.

Nick pretended he was grazing. Jeff stepped out into the circle and promptly fell down. On purpose.

On the sidelines, there was clapping.

Ally looked out of the holes in the back of the horse and saw Miss Kruck standing on the rim of the circle. "You guys'll do great!"

Jeff clowned it up, and soon they were all working on a routine. Jeff said, "We'll have to practice it. I'll enter us in the contest, though."

"Contest!" Ally cried.

"Yeah, best new talent," Jeff said.

"It's a lot of fun," Miss Kruck added as they took off their costumes and sat down on the curb.

After a snack, Ally was eager to get back to the skating, but Jeff said he had to go by the stables and clean them out. Nick and Ally went with him, and soon they were having a fine time brushing down the horses after a quick ride.

Ally and Nick then went home for dinner. Once dinner was over, they stepped out into the evening air for a walk and found themselves meandering up the street.

"We're going in the direction of Jeff's house," Nick said with a hint of aggravation in his voice.

"I wasn't really thinking about it."

"Do we have to hang out with him every minute?"

"No," Ally answered. "But I thought you were starting to like him."

"He's okay. It's just that . . ."

"What?"

Nick shrugged. "Nothing. Let's just go see if Jeff is out and about."

They stepped around behind some houses. Jeff's house was only a few houses down. Ally suddenly spotted a figure run across the back lawn and disappear into the woods.

She grabbed Nick and made him duck down.

"What?" Nick asked.

"I think it was Jeff darting into the trees."

"So what?"

"Let's see where he was going."

"You mean spy on him?"

"No, just follow him. Come on."

They hurried down to where they saw Jeff run into the trees. Ally quickly found the well-worn path, one that she'd never been on before.

"This must be it," she whispered.

They walked cautiously down the trail as Ally searched the trees for signs of Jeff. A few minutes later, she saw him climbing a rope ladder. She motioned to Nick, and they stopped and crouched, watching.

"What is it?" Ally whispered, pointing to where Jeff was climbing.

"Looks like a tree fort," Nick answered. "Let's circle around behind it to get a better look."

"Oh, so now you're interested?"

"Okay, maybe I don't mind being a spy sometimes."

"Or a P.I."

"P.I.?"

"Private investigator."

"Do you think Jeff is the one wrecking the houses?" Nick asked suddenly.

"No, I don't think so," Ally said. "I'm just having fun. Let's go. If he comes back, he'll come back this way."

They crept around through the thick woods to the other side of the tree fort, keeping it in sight but shielding themselves so Jeff couldn't see them. Fifteen minutes later, Jeff climbed down from the tree fort, looked around, and then hurried off back toward the houses.

"Are you thinking what I'm thinking?" Nick said.

"What?"

"Go check it out?"

"Let's."

Nine

The Mystery at the Tree Fort

The tree fort was built of what looked like scrap wood from the many house-building sites in the area. It looked kind of ramshackle, but strong enough to hold both of them. After making sure Jeff was gone, Nick climbed the ladder. Ally followed.

Inside the tree fort, they found a number of interesting things lying around. A box with a lot of canned and packaged food lay in one corner. Next to it sat a bunch of camping gear, as if someone were planning a trip. In another corner stood a large bag of oats.

But the real revelation was a pile of VCRs, tape decks, and other pieces of electronic equipment. They looked old and used, but that didn't mean they couldn't have been stolen.

Nick glanced at Ally unhappily. "Do you think what I think?"

"That he steals this from the houses?"

"Exactly."

"Let's get out of here."

They climbed down and stole off through the trees, taking another route toward the creek and the Matthews's farm to make sure they didn't run into Jeff. When they reached the road, they saw a house with a car Ally recognized parked in front. They watched as Mr. Bell stepped out of the house, shut the door, and walked to his car. Nick and Ally hurried across the street.

"Mr. Bell! Mr. Bell!"

Mr. Bell looked startled, but then regained his composure. "Oh, it's you kids."

"Did someone trash another house?"

"That's what it looks like. I was just going to call the police." Mr. Bell grabbed a cell phone out of his car.

"I'm sorry," Ally said. "I hope they catch these people."

"We'll get them. We're pretty sure it's kids."

"Do you suspect anyone in particular?" Nick asked.

"Some kid trying to fence electronic items, probably. You don't know any likely suspects, do you?" Mr. Bell dialed his phone.

Ally glanced at Nick and took a breath. "Not really."

"Well, don't go snooping around. These people could be dangerous." He spoke into the phone. "Yes, I'd like to report a break-in." He turned to Nick and Ally. "I'll take care of this, kids. Thanks for your cooperation."

"Anytime," Ally said.

"Glad to be of service," Nick added.

They walked off as Mr. Bell spoke with the police. When they were out of earshot, they snapped into a faster walk.

"What are we going to do, Nick?"

"About Jeff?"

"What else? He could be the one doing the robberies. If we stop him before he gets caught, it would be much easier on him."

"Yeah, he'd only go to jail for twenty years instead of thirty."

"Do you think it could be that bad?"

"I don't know," Nick answered. "Kids don't really go to jail. He'd probably end up in juvenile detention. But I don't think it'll be good any way you cut it."

"What should we do then?"

"I don't know."

"Look," Ally said. "I think we need to work this one out before we tell anyone. We don't want to betray Jeff."

"I guess I agree with that."

"You guess?"

"Yeah. I'm with you in not going to the police or anything, at least not until we're sure. But I think we should at least confront Jeff."

"I hate this. I just hate it."

Ten

Hound Dog

The next day, Ally was determined to talk to Jeff more directly about the break-ins, but she wasn't sure how he would handle it, especially when he found out they had been in his tree house. Still, she had to know what Jeff was doing. For his sake more than anyone else's.

She met up with Nick that morning. As they walked up the road to Jeff's house, Ally spotted him ambling down toward them. He waved.

"Let me handle it, Nick, okay?" Ally said.

"Fine with me," Nick answered.

Jeff hurried up to them. "Hey, Coombsie has a surprise for us. Want to see it?"

"What is it?" Ally asked cautiously. "Not more ghosts?"

"He's sorry about all that," Jeff said. "He doesn't know why or how it comes over him. He just loses control when he thinks they're there. But I think it'll be okay. He says it's really cool what he's found."

So they followed Jeff toward Coombsie's place in the woods. Ally tried to think of a way of confronting Jeff.

"We saw Mr. Bell today," she said.

"Who's he?" Jeff asked.

"The owner of some rental houses. Another house was broken into."

"Man, how many is it now?" Jeff asked with what seemed like honest amazement. Ally wasn't sure how to proceed.

"I think it's just a few. You're sure Coombsie isn't involved, Jeff?"

"Well, I don't know for sure, but I haven't ever seen anything at his cabin that looked stolen. Why do you think Coombsie would do that kind of thing, anyway?"

"Just wondering." Ally chewed her lip. "The burglars are stealing electronic stuff out of the houses. Stereos. VCRs. That kind of thing."

"You can go to the local dump for that," Jeff said.

"What do you mean?" Ally felt Nick leaning forward with interest.

"You know, the dump we were near the other day when we saw the dogs. It's way over on the other side of where Coombsie lives. Coombsie and I have been over there; you can find all kinds of stuff."

"Like what?"

"VCRs. Refrigerators. Most of them are no good, I'm sure. But some might work. People throw away everything these days." Jeff hurried on ahead. "I can't wait to see Coombsie's surprise. He finds the coolest things."

As Jeff walked out in front of them, Ally whispered to Nick, "He doesn't act guilty at all, does he?"

"Maybe he isn't, Ally."

"But what about all that stuff, those electronic things at the tree fort?"

"Hurry up," Jeff called. "I'm leaving you in the dust."

Ally stopped and regarded Nick with firm eyes. "What do you think? Come on, what should we do?"

"Just hang in there for awhile. We'll get it out of him."

"You think so?"

"Hurry up!" Jeff yelled again.

"We better get moving," Nick said to Ally, then took off running.

They caught up to Jeff as he waited in a copse of laurel and pine trees.

"You know, I wouldn't question Coombsie about the break-ins. He might not like you suspecting him of something like that," Jeff said. "He's kind of sensitive about honesty."

"It was just a question," Ally said, noting that she sounded a little defensive.

"Accusing someone of something—that's nasty," Jeff said. "Especially when they're innocent."

"I wasn't accusing him," Ally said, narrowing her eyes.

"I bet you even suspect me," Jeff said suddenly, looking from Ally to Nick and then back. "I bet you do, don't you?"

"It's just that I don't know you very well," Ally said. "I mean, you yourself said it must be someone who lives in the area."

"So you think it's me, don't you?"

"I didn't say that."

"Do you, Nick?" Jeff asked, looking to Nick.

Nick shook his head. "I hardly know you, Jeff. You could be a thief for all I know."

"Thanks a lot."

"Look, just tell us then and that'll settle it," Ally said. "Do you have anything to do with the break-ins?"

"No."

"Well, that's good enough for me," Nick said.

"And you?" Jeff asked Ally. He stared her down, his eyes not blinking. He looked angry and hurt. She knew she couldn't bring up the tree fort now. Not yet. Not until she was sure.

"I believe anyone's word until it's proven otherwise," Ally answered. She moved uncomfortably from foot to foot.

"I believe anyone, period." Jeff said angrily. "I believe they tell the truth if they tell me it's the truth." Jeff stared at them for a moment, then shrugged. "No, I don't really. Most people are liars, and if you don't believe me, I guess I can live with that. But I am telling you the truth."

"Then what about the—?" Ally caught herself and stopped.

"What about what?"

"You and Coombsie. Where does he fit into the Jeff Reynolds life story?"

Jeff grinned. "Coombsie has never betrayed me, and he never would. I can trust him completely."

"Is that what you want from people?"

Jeff just shrugged. Then he turned to look down the trail. "Come on. If we keep this up, it'll be tomorrow by the time we get there."

They hurried along until they found Coombsie's cabin. Jeff walked right up to the door and pounded on it. There was no answer. Then Coombsie came around the side of the house with a rifle in his hand.

"Hey, we came to see this surprise you have," Jeff said.

Coombsie looked sleepy to Ally, and he rubbed his eyes as if he was just waking up.

"Been taking a pine tree nap," Coombsie said. "Fell asleep trying to get me some rabbit for dinner."

"Coombsie likes to fall asleep in the boughs of a pine tree over a ways," Jeff explained. "It's very nice. Kind of sways in the wind."

"It sounds relaxing," Ally said.

"So what's the surprise?" Jeff asked Coombsie.

"Follow me," Coombsie answered. He dumped the gun, picked up his violin case, and handed Jeff a flashlight.

"What's this for?"

"You'll see."

The three of them followed Coombsie up a trail into the trees. A few minutes later, they stood in front of the mouth of a fairly large cave carved into a wall of rock.

"What's in there?" Jeff asked.

"Come and see," Coombsie said, ducking down under the top lip of the cave and stepping inside.

"It's not a bear, is it?" Jeff said.

"Come and see," Coombsie said, grinning. His red lips against the gray and black of his beard reminded Ally of a smiling Santa.

"It isn't a bear, is it?" Ally said nervously.

"Yeah, and Coombsie's going to give it a concert," Nick said.

Coombsie had already disappeared inside. Jeff pulled the flashlight out of his pocket. "C'mon. Let's go," he said.

When they were inside, they found Coombsie, standing and listening. "Whatever you do, don't startle them," he said. And don't run."

"But what is it?" Ally said, her eyes widening.

"Just come," Coombsie said. "Don't you like a little adventure?"

"Sure, but . . ."

Jeff stepped past her behind Coombsie and tramped on into the cave. Ally took a deep breath and followed, with Nick behind her. A moment later, she heard a soft mewling sound, like a deer or a fawn in pain. When they came around a corner under an outcropping of rock, Jeff shone the light ahead and Coombsie stopped.

Ally heard barking.

"It's okay, girl," Coombsie said gently.

Ally looked down the line of light from the flashlight. It settled on a small mound of leaves and pine boughs. On the mound rested a dog. It looked like a black lab to Ally.

"Had the pups about six weeks ago," Coombsie said. "Been bringing her food every day. One of the dump dogs, I suppose."

As Ally's eyes adjusted to the light, she saw a small pile of fluffy pups who all appeared to be asleep, except one, which was crawling desperately over the others.

"I call her Shea," Coombsie said, pointing to the mother. "I don't know what her real name is."

He walked to the dog and crouched down beside her, rubbing her back.

The other puppies woke up and began hustling over one another in a moving pile. Coombsie took some bits of food out of his pocket and gave it to the mother. "Pups're too young for real food."

He rubbed the mother dog all over and talked to her as the kids looked on. Then Ally knelt down by the pups and began petting them. "They're so cute," she said.

Nick picked one up, and it wet on him.

"Figures I'd get the one that had to go," he said, setting the tiny dog down.

Coombsie laughed a deep, kettledrum kind of laugh. It was the first time Ally had ever heard him actually laugh.

"So this is the surprise?" Jeff said, stooping and touching a pup.

"No, this is the surprise," Coombsie said, picking up his violin. He removed it from the case and set it to his neck and chin. Then he began to play Brahms's "Lullaby."

At first, it was just the bare melody. Da-da-da. Da-da-da. Da-da-da-da-da-da-da . . . Then he added in his own riffs and ad libs to the lullaby.

Shea sat up and began to yowl with the melody. The puppies then gathered around the mother, making their own squealing noises.

Coombsie's eyes twinkled. "They're my choir," he said over the lilting of the violin. He slowly brought the music to a stop. Shea lay back down and turned on her side to suckle the puppies.

"Better leave her now," Coombsie said, packing up the violin. "A dog like this values its privacy."

"Like you, Coombsie?" Jeff said.

"Yeah, like me," Coombsie said, leading them to the outcrop and out of the cave.

"That was incredible," Ally said when they stood back in the sunlight.

Coombsie replied, "All part of getting back to nature. I wish I was one of them. They have the real life."

"It'll get better, Coombsie," Jeff said. "I know it."

"Yeah."

They all walked in silence back to the cabin, then Nick said they'd better be getting home. Jeff said his aunt and he had to go into town that afternoon, so Ally and Nick walked along the trail to the main road alone, leaving Jeff behind.

"I think Coombsie is a very gentle person," Ally said as they stepped onto the main road.

"I think things like that dog and Jeff keep him sane," Nick added, nodding.

Ally looked at Nick with admiration. "That's a good thought, and maybe that's part of the answer for Coombsie."

"Jeff too," Nick said without explaining himself further.

When they reached Ally's house, Nick said he'd better get on home and check on Molly. Ally was glad to be alone. She had a lot to think about: *Am I wrong to suspect that Jeff could be the house robber?*

Eleven

Caught Red-Handed

As Ally stepped inside the house, her mother called to her from the kitchen.

"Guess who's coming over for dinner tonight?"

"I don't know. Who?" Ally said without much curiosity. She felt tired and upset about not getting things straight with Jeff.

"Your friend Jeff and his aunt."

"You're kidding." Ally perked up.

"I called his aunt up. She's very nice. She wants to meet us."

"That's cool."

Ally walked directly to the phone, picked it up, and dialed Nick's number. When Molly answered, she asked for Nick, and he came on seconds later.

"Hey!" he said.

"Look, we've got to go back to that tree fort," Ally whispered. "We have to get this straightened out before tonight."

"Why? What's tonight?"

"Just trust me on it. I'll meet you on the road."

Ally hung up and walked into the kitchen. "I'm just going for a walk with Nick, Mom," she said.

"Fine. Be back by 4:00. I'll need some help. They're coming over at 6:00."

"No problem."

৩৩

Ally met up with Nick and the two of them hurried past Jeff's house through the trees so they wouldn't be seen. Ally saw that Miss Kruck's car was gone, so she and Jeff had probably gone into town.

"What's the rush, anyway?" Nick asked, struggling to keep up with Ally.

"If Jeff is doing this, maybe it'll be easier if we talk to him tonight with his aunt there. I don't know. I just feel we've got to get it settled."

"Okay, I'm with you."

They found the tree fort, undisturbed and quiet. Ally climbed the rope ladder first. Nick followed. This time she gave the contents of the tree fort a much closer inspection. She found a sleeping bag, a knapsack with various camping items in it, and what appeared to be several old flashlights. There was the stack of electronic devices in one corner. She looked at them closely. None appeared new. Several looked pretty beat up.

"What could he do with these?" Ally asked Nick as he rummaged through the sacks of oats and other items.

Nick answered, "Remember, Mr. Bell said they 'fence' the electronic stuff."

"What is 'fence'?"

"I think it's like selling them to people who can get stolen items back into the mainstream. Middlemen, I guess, who can then sell the stuff for real."

"What would he use the money for?"

"Go live somewhere else?" Nick answered, studying a pair of riding boots. "He doesn't seem to like living with Miss Kruck that much."

"You think he wants to go live with his father?"

"That could be it. But where is his father?"

"We don't know." Ally picked up a VCR and pushed her finger into the slot. There was a tape lodged in it.

"There's a tape in this one."

"Well, that pretty much proves it," Nick said.

"What?"

"Would someone throw away a VCR with a tape in it?"

"What are you thinking?"

"I was thinking Jeff might have found these things at the landfill or some place. But with a tape still in it . . ."

"Maybe it's just stuck. Maybe the VCR died with the tape in it."

"Died with its boots on, huh?"

"Cute." She set it back down and sighed. "If Jeff is the one doing this, we should persuade him to return all the stuff. That way, they might not press charges."

"But what about him tearing up the houses? There was a lot of damage."

"Rats. I forgot about that."

A stick broke outside, and Nick and Ally froze. Ally scurried to the window and looked out.

"Oh no!" she whispered. "It's Jeff!"

"What do we do?" Nick set down the boots and stared at Ally with fear on his face. "He's real uptight about people betraying him."

"Okay, this is my fault. I'll just say—oh, man, I'd have to lie."

"That might be better than telling him we're spying on him."

Another stick cracked, and the sound of someone brushing through the branches came closer.

"Okay, I'll do the talking," Ally whispered. "God, please give me something to say!"

They heard Jeff grab the rope ladder. He started climbing upward. Before he reached the top, he shoved a VCR through the hole in the floor into the tree fort. Ally stared at it, then prayed for God to give her the words to say.

"Hey, Jeff!"

Ally jerked. The voice came from outside. She froze and listened intently.

"Jeff, whatcha doin'?"

It was Coombsie.

"Hey, Coombsie, what're you doing here?"

"Just practicin' my violin."

Jeff's hand disappeared from the hole, and he climbed down the rope ladder.

"What's up?"

"Just hangin' around. Want to see something cool?" Ally heard Coombsie say.

"Sure. I'm not busy."

Coombsie and Jeff began to walk away. Ally nervously stepped to the window and looked out. As she peered out the window, Coombsie turned around and caught her eye.

His eyes narrowed, but then he winked and turned back to Jeff. Ally watched them vanish into the depths of the woods.

Ally closed her eyes briefly. "Thanks, Lord. That was close."

"It's a good thing Coombsie came along," Nick said.

"I wonder how he happened to be there? Nick, you'll never believe this, but when I looked out the window, he turned and winked at me."

"So he knows we're here."

"I guess." Ally was silent for a moment. "I don't want Jeff to think we've betrayed him, but I think he's lying to us," she finally said. "I just don't think we have the evidence to prove it."

"So what do we do?"

"Get out of here, first, before he comes back."

Nick glanced down at the VCR. "Well, I guess we'll find out if another house was broken into today. This could be from it."

"Yeah, let's go call Mr. Bell."

Twelve

The Call

"Is this Mr. Bell?" Ally asked into the phone as Nick stood beside her at his house.

"Yes, who is this?"

"Ally O'Connor." Ally nodded at Nick. "Look, I was just wondering. There hasn't been another break-in, has there?"

"Not that I know of. Why, do you know something?"

"No, not really. Just wondering. We're trying to be vigilant is all."

"If I find out about one, I'll let you know. But I can tell you that we're closing in on someone."

"Oh, really?" Ally asked, trying to sound casual.

"Yeah, a kid who lives down the way from your street. Kind of a roughneck."

"Oh, who is he?"

"Can't say at this point. But we've got him in our sights."

"Well, that . . . is a relief," Ally said, giving Nick a look.

"Yes, it is. And thanks for your help," Mr. Bell said and hung up.

Ally stood there with her eyes closed, feeling overwhelmed and terrified for Jeff.

"What's up?" Nick asked.

"They think they've got someone—a boy who lives nearby."

"Oh, man. Jeff, right?"

"Yeah, I would guess that. Mr. Bell didn't give me a name."

"Man, Ally, we've got to do something."

Ally glanced at her watch. "Mom is having Jeff and Miss Kruck over for dinner tonight. Maybe I can try to talk to Jeff again then."

"Good idea. I'll be praying."

Ally left Nick's house, full of anxiety about that night.

Jeff and Miss Kruck arrived at the O'Connors at precisely 6:00. Ally greeted them at the door and led them into the house. "My mom's in the kitchen and Dad's in the study," she said to Miss Kruck. "Jeff, you can sit out here. We'll be ready for dinner in a few minutes."

Jeff sat down and said, "I could go for something to drink."

"Coke, ginger ale, orange juice?"

"Coke'll be fine."

Ally stepped into the kitchen to get a couple of drinks for her and Jeff. Miss Kruck and her mother talked animatedly about cooking, and it sounded to Ally like Miss Kruck really liked learning new recipes.

She returned to the family room and sat down across from Jeff.

"So what're you so quiet about?" Jeff said after taking a sip of Coke.

"Nothing," Ally replied, wishing her mother would hurry up with dinner. "I'm just a little nervous about having you over is all."

Jeff grinned. "Hey, don't be. We're friends, right?"

"Yeah." Ally knew she should just plunge right in. "Jeff, I talked to Mr. Bell today."

"Who's he?"

"I told you. The man who's involved with these house break-ins."

"Oh, that again. Man, can you lay off it? I'm not the person. Coombsie isn't the person. You're relentless!"

"Well, I just wanted you to know what he said. They think they've got the person identified, and they're ready to close in on him soon."

"Cool. That'll put it behind us."

Ally studied Jeff's face, trying to see if he was telling the truth or not. He just smiled back at her with a friendly expression. If he was lying, he was the best liar she'd ever encountered.

"You still think I'm doing it, don't you?" Jeff said coldly, his friendly expression changing. "It's beginning to put a real crimp in our relationship."

Voices from the kitchen resounded in the hall, and Miss Kruck and Ally's mom walked in carrying plates. "Dinner's ready, folks. Ally, would you go call your father?" Mrs. O'Connor said.

Ally jumped up, wishing she had the courage to bring up the tree fort and its evidence. She had to find the right time and place and just get it out. But when?

She hurried down the hall to her dad's study and told him dinner was ready.

With gusto everyone dug into the spaghetti Mrs. O'Connor had prepared. Everyone except Ally. She kept listening for the slightest piece of incriminating evidence in Jeff's words.

Meanwhile, her mom and dad kept up a battery of questions for Miss Kruck. Jeff even chimed in, not being closed and angry like he'd been in some other situations. He seemed to be enjoying himself. At several points in the conversation, Jeff talked about roller-blading. He reminded Ally that they had to practice their carnival routine for several hours before the actual event.

Deep down, though, Ally worried that Jeff wouldn't be at the carnival. He'd be in juvenile detention.

⁊

The phone rang at about 8:00, just as Miss Kruck and Jeff were leaving. Ally picked it up.

"Hello?"

"Hello. This is Mr. Bell. To whom am I speaking?"

"This is Ally."

"Oh, hello. Well, I just wanted to let you know there's been another break-in," Mr. Bell said. "A number of things taken, and the house really beat up."

"I'm sorry," Ally said.

"Look, Ally, I know you're a good kid and everything," Mr. Bell intoned. "But if you know something about this, I think you should come out with it."

"I would if I could," Ally said. "But thanks for letting me know."

"All right, but there is such a thing as being a conspirator or an accessory to a crime, Ally. I'd hate to see you charged with something for withholding information."

"Mr. Bell, I really . . ."

Everyone was staring at her, obviously wondering what this conversation was about. Jeff's eyes on her felt like daggers.

"We've got company, Mr. Bell," Ally said quickly. "I'm going to have to go. I'll let you know about anything I find out, though."

"Good. Have a nice evening."

Ally hung up.

"What on earth was that all about, honey?" Mrs. O'Connor said.

"Oh, he just told me there's been another break-in."
Ally's eyes were on Jeff. She sensed his dismay.

"And why is he telling you?"

"I asked him today if there'd been any more, that's all.
I'm kind of interested. That's all. It *is* our neighborhood."

"Let the police do their work, honey," Mr. O'Connor
said. "They'll get to the bottom of it. You don't need to get
involved."

Mrs. O'Connor turned to Miss Kruck. "It was certainly
nice meeting you, Babs. I hope you'll feel free to come by
anytime."

"Oh, of course," Miss Kruck said. "I'm so glad Jeff and
Ally have become friends."

Ally could still feel Jeff's eyes on her, but she didn't look
at him.

"Thank you, again, for a great dinner and talk and
everything," Miss Kruck was saying. "I'll have to have you
over sometime soon."

"That would be great. Bye, now," Mrs. O'Connor said.

Jeff said good-bye and walked out the door with Miss
Kruck. The moment they were gone, Mrs. O'Connor
turned to Ally.

"What is going on here, young lady?"

Ally hung her head. "I think Jeff is the one doing the
break-ins."

"Why?"

"Just some things I've found out."

"Like what? That's a serious accusation, Ally."

"I know. I know!"

"Then what evidence do you have?" Mr. O'Connor said.

Ally suddenly burst into tears. "I'm sorry. I'm sorry. I
just have to think about this."

She dashed from the room and jumped onto her bed,
burying her head in the pillow.

Seconds later, Mrs. O'Connor stood by the bed. She sat
down and caressed Ally's hair. "I'm sure you have good

reasons for this, Ally. But be sure you're not making too many assumptions, okay?"

Ally nodded into the pillow.

"Jeff seems like a very nice boy."

"He is, Mom. He is."

"Then why do you suspect him?"

Ally rolled over, took a deep breath, and told her mother about the tree fort.

"Boy, that does sound serious," Mrs. O'Connor said when Ally was done. "Let's pray about this, okay? That's the best thing to do when you're faced with a troubling situation."

"I know, Mom. But what can I do besides pray? Should I talk to Jeff? I just don't want him to think I've betrayed him."

"You're trying to help him, honey. That's all this is."

"But he's got this thing about being betrayed. It's really a big deal with him."

"We'll work it out, okay? Let's pray first."

"Okay."

Ally bowed her head, and Mrs. O'Connor prayed for Jeff and his aunt. When she concluded, Mrs. O'Connor said, "Feel any better?"

"A little."

"Well, get some rest. I'll call Jeff's aunt tomorrow—I'd like to get to know her a little better. Maybe she can come over for tea."

"All right, Mom. Thanks."

"Sleep well, honey."

Mrs. O'Connor left, and Ally got her pajamas on and brushed her teeth. Then she crawled into bed and closed her eyes. "Lord, please help this whole thing. That's all I know to pray. Amen."

She tossed and turned for over an hour until exhaustion set in and she fell asleep.

Thirteen

A Meeting of the Hearts

Ally puttered around the house the next morning until Nick came by. There was a phone call at about 11:00 that Mrs. O'Connor answered. When she finished, she walked into the family room where Nick and Ally sat sipping Cokes and talking.

"That was Mr. Bell. He says the police are going to do a stakeout of some of the houses."

Ally gave Nick a worried look. But she was glad Miss Kruck was coming over later that day. Maybe she would tell them something about Jeff.

Miss Kruck came by at 2:00, and Mrs. O'Connor offered her a cup of tea. Then she, Ally, and Nick sat down with her to talk.

They talked about the weather, their gardens, and recent summer vacations. After a half hour had passed, Ally began getting antsy. She wanted to talk about Jeff. She was just about to bring up the subject when Miss Kruck did it for her.

"I'm so glad you two have become friends with Jeff," Miss Kruck said, looking at Ally and Nick.

"We're glad too," Ally said. "Jeff's a good guy."

"Jeff needs good friends like you." Miss Kruck turned to Mrs. O'Connor. "Jeff's had some difficulty adjusting to living with me. I suppose he's told the kids that he lived with his father?"

Ally and Nick nodded their heads.

"Well, I feel it's important for you to know a little bit about Jeff's background. Jeff can be difficult, but I don't want you to think he's a bad kid." Miss Kruck took a deep breath. "Jeff's father—my brother, Steven—was getting into trouble from the time he was a teenager. By the time Jeff was born, he was into drugs and had landed into jail. So when Jeff's mother died, Jeff came to live with me. Then, when Steven got out of jail, Jeff went back to live with him. He lived with his father until just recently, because my brother's in jail again."

"Oh, how awful for Jeff!" Mrs. O'Connor said sympathetically, reaching for Miss Kruck's hand and giving it a squeeze.

"I know," Miss Kruck said. "That's why I try to be understanding when Jeff gets . . . difficult. He doesn't like my rules and my asking him questions. But I'm just trying to be a good parent, or whatever it is I am." Miss Kruck sniffled. "I'm sorry. I'm sorry." She picked up a napkin and blew her nose in it. "I should've brought some Kleenex. . . . Look, I don't expect you to solve Jeff's problems. He's a decent kid. He just wants to . . . not live with me is about it in a nutshell."

"I'm sorry," Mrs. O'Connor said, touching Miss Kruck's hand again.

"If Jeff doesn't live with you, who would he live with then?"

"Oh, he has this crazy idea that he'll get his father out of jail and they'll be back together and all will be bliss. It's never going to happen. His father's in for ten more years without parole. He did a lot more than just deal drugs. I'm trying to make it sound as good as I can, but it's really very horrible. I just wish I could make Jeff understand how much I really care about him."

"I'm so sorry," Mrs. O'Connor said. "Please let us know if there is anything we can do to help."

Miss Kruck smiled. "Thank you. I really appreciate that. Well, I better be off. I'm going on my weekly visit to the sundae shop. It's my one culinary pleasure in the week so I make a trip of it."

"Well, why don't we all go?" Mrs. O'Connor said. "I could use a sundae myself. What do you say Ally? Nick?"

"I don't have any money," Nick said.

Ally laughed. "You never have any money. I think my mom'll pay for you, Nick."

"No, I'll pay for everyone. It'll be a treat," Miss Kruck said. "Let's go. I'd love it."

"We're there then," Mrs. O'Connor said. Seconds later, they all piled into Miss Kruck's car and headed for town.

Miss Kruck had everyone sit at the counter. The man behind the counter said, "So what'll it be today, Babs?"

"These three want sundaes, Gene. I'll have my usual."

Gene turned to Mrs. O'Connor and Ally. "What kind of sundaes, ladies?"

Ally said, "I'll have hot fudge with chocolate chip ice cream."

Mrs. O'Connor added, "I'll have chocolate chip with lots of whipped cream."

Nick ordered a hot fudge sundae, and soon everyone was eating in bliss. The ice cream was thick, heavy, and full of flavor. Ally hadn't known about this place, but she decided she wouldn't mind coming down here once a week with Miss Kruck for the rest of her life.

While they ate, Miss Kruck regaled them with stories about Jeff from the time he was two. She soon had everyone laughing.

"You know, sometimes it's hard to make a little boy understand what going in the toilet is all about. I tried pouring water out of a jar into the toilet, all kinds of things. One day I thought he had it. He went in the toilet like a big boy. I gave him a standing ovation. But the next day, he said he had to go, so I told him to go. And he just went there right on the floor!"

"You really have some great memories, Babs," Mrs. O'Connor said, laughing.

"It's been fun, since I never had children of my own. Jeff was two when I started taking care of him. And then his dad got out of prison and wanted him back. So Jeff was with him for several years. He came back to me at the beginning of this summer. And even though Jeff can be difficult, it's good to have him back."

They finished the sundaes and walked back out to the car. Ally thought it was the most fun she'd had in months. But she kept thinking that they should tell Miss Kruck about the tree fort. She worried, though, about how Miss Kruck would take it. She seemed very protective of Jeff.

Ally was still worrying about telling Miss Kruck about the tree fort when she saw a man up ahead hitchhiking. She recognized Coombsie immediately.

"It's Coombsie!" she cried.

"You know him?" Miss Kruck asked, slowing down.

"It's Jeff's friend, Mr. Coombs."

"Oh, that's wonderful," Miss Kruck said. "I've heard so much about him." She stopped right in front of Coombsie, and he ran to the window to look in. He was carrying his violin case.

Fourteen

Clicking

Miss Kruck leaned over the front seat and said, "So you're the famous Mr. Coombs. Would you like a ride?"

"Be much obliged, Ma'am."

When Coombsie opened the back door, he laughed. "Ally! Nick! What's this?"

"We're with Jeff's aunt," Ally said as Coombsie sat in the rear seat of the car. "And this is my mom."

Mrs. O'Connor swiveled around and extended her hand. "Pleased to meet you, Mr. Coombs. Call me Liz."

Miss Kruck held out her hand, and when Coombsie took it, he said, "Jeff didn't tell me you were such a lovely looking lady."

"Oh, he would never say that about me," she answered, blushing.

"Well, he should've."

Ally glanced from Miss Kruck to Coombsie, then gave her mother a look.

"So where should I let you off?" Miss Kruck asked.

"Up by the old Gibbs place, if you please."

Thinking about doing a little matchmaking, Ally said, "Oh, you should come over to Miss Kruck's house sometime, Coombsie. You could play your violin for her. I bet she'd love it."

"You play the violin?" Miss Kruck asked.

Coombsie held up the case. "Sort of."

"He's a pro," Nick said, grinning at Ally.

"Well, I would love to hear you play. I play violin too. Maybe we can—"

"Do a duet!" Ally cried.

"Sure, I guess so," Coombsie said.

"Well, then it's settled," Miss Kruck said. "You're coming over for dinner, and Liz, you and Ally and Nick are all invited too. I stuck a roast in the oven before I came over to your house, thinking I'd eat it over the next month. Now I won't have to worry about that."

"Great," Ally said and sat back, watching Coombsie's eyes. He hadn't taken them off Miss Kruck since he'd gotten into the car. And even though he was looking mostly at the back of her head, Ally could see something was changing in Coombsie. *Could Miss Kruck be the answer to my prayer for Coombsie's mental health?*

Miss Kruck told them to be at her house at 5:30 sharp. When they all arrived at her house, Coombsie was polishing his violin in the living room while Jeff sat there looking miserable. A second violin lay on a chair.

Everyone sat down in the living room, and Miss Kruck served some hors d'oeuvres of bacon-wrapped scallops, a cheese ball and crackers, eggnog and punch. She was dressed in a mauve-colored skirt with a cream-white blouse. She looked stunning. Next to her, Coombsie's face was radiant in a way that Ally had never imagined it could be. He seemed charged with electricity, making his way around the house, helping Miss Kruck with this and that like he'd been there for a century.

Miss Kruck, after giving everyone time to consume most of the delicious treats, invited them all to the dining room. She then served a fine dinner of roast beef, baked potatoes, creamed spinach, candied carrots, and scrumptious rolls and butter.

The dinner conversation was fun, with everyone joining in and laughing. Everyone, that is, except Jeff. He seemed angry that Coombsie was acting so "in love" with his aunt. Twice he whispered to Ally, "He has no idea what she's really like." But Ally considered the possibility of a relationship between the two a gift of God and told Jeff so.

When dinner was completed, Miss Kruck invited everyone to sit down for a concert. "Coombsie and I have prepared a list of things you might enjoy. I think you'll find that we are a natural dynamic duo."

This comment brought a heavy sigh from Jeff, but everyone else thought it funny.

Then the duet started. Ally had never heard anything like it. They went through contemporary numbers, like songs by the Beatles and Elvis Presley, then went on to various musical tunes from *The Sound of Music, The Music Man,* and several others, and finally ended up with a few classical numbers. The sound was marvelous. Mrs. O'Connor suggested several times that they go on the road and "make a million dollars."

When they were done, they both sat down, panting. Coombsie said to Miss Kruck, "Jeff never told me you could play."

Miss Kruck laughed. "I don't think Jeff likes to talk about me that much."

"Why didn't you tell me about this, fella?" Coombsie asked Jeff.

Jeff simply shrugged. "I didn't think you'd be interested."

"Interested in Babs? Why wouldn't I be? She's a great lady."

Miss Kruck blushed.

Coombsie then told more of his stories, both fiction and nonfiction, and kept everyone laughing and crying for more till 10:00. Only Jeff remained unmoved. Ally figured it was probably difficult for him to accept that his aunt, whom he wanted to get away from, was becoming so chummy with his best friend.

Ally knew too that this wasn't the time to bring up the tree fort. The discussion had to be when Jeff was in a better mood.

After a fine dessert of chocolate mousse, the O'Connors and Nick left for home. Miss Kruck offered to give Coombsie a ride, but he said he could find his way. She kept telling him, "Please come by again. We'll do a dueling violins reunion."

Coombsie promised more than once, "I will, I will."

On the way up the street—the O'Connors had walked from their house earlier in the evening—Ally said to Coombsie, "I think she likes you, Coombsie."

"You think so? I might have to shave off my beard."

"She likes that too," Nick added.

"I don't know," Coombsie said. "These things never work out for me."

"Ask her out for tomorrow night," Ally blurted.

"Ally," her mother chided, "Coombsie can work out his own romantic life."

Coombsie shook his head. "Well, I don't know about that." He smiled at the group. "Well, here's where I turn off."

"Really, Coombsie, ask her out," Ally said again.

Coombsie paused by the trees on the side of the road. "Maybe," he said, and dashed into the trees and disappeared.

Ally, Nick, and her parents continued on. "They are so fun," Mrs. O'Connor said, looking up into the moonlight.

"Jeff was kind of quiet, though," Nick said.

"He's probably not used to Coombsie showing an interest in women, and his Aunt Babs showing an interest in

Coombsie," Mr. O'Connor said. "Reminds me of my younger days." He gave Mrs. O'Connor a kiss on the lips.

They walked in silence for awhile, then suddenly Ally said, "But I'm bummed that I didn't get a chance to talk to Jeff about the robberies."

"Darling," Mrs. O'Connor said, "I think Jeff is fine. I don't think you have to worry about anything. Let's just pray that God will take care of this situation."

"Then what about the tree fort?"

"I don't know, honey. Maybe you can talk to Jeff tomorrow. And then you can let the police do their job; they'll catch who's doing this."

"Yeah, I guess so."

Fifteen

In the Jaws of the Trap

The next morning, Jeff, Ally, and Nick practiced the carnival routine again in the circle, but then Ally didn't see Jeff the rest of the day or the next day. By the next night, she was worried. She finally called Miss Kruck at 7:00 in the evening, and Miss Kruck said Jeff had gone out after dinner to tend to the horses.

As usual, Nick was sitting in the living room talking to Mr. O'Connor about sports. Ally stepped in and said, "Nick, want to go for a walk?"

Mrs. O'Connor immediately interrupted. "Oh, we were going to take you into town for dessert, honey. We thought we might hit that ice cream parlor again."

Ally frowned at Nick, trying to communicate that they had more important things to do. "I don't really feel like going tonight," she said. "I'm kind of ice creamed out."

"Me too," Nick piped up.

"What?" Mrs. O'Connor answered. "I can't believe what I'm hearing! You two love ice cream. You especially, Nick."

Nick touched his forehead. "You know, I have a terrible headache. Ice cream wouldn't do it any good."

"Take some aspirin. What is with you guys?"

"Okay," Ally huffed, "we'll go already!"

So everyone stepped out of the house and into the O'Connors' car. It was still light out, and as they drove, Ally spotted a figure on the road.

"It's Jeff," Ally said. "Let's invite him too."

Mr. O'Connor slowed to a stop, and Mrs. O'Connor rolled down her window. "Jeff, would you like to come with us to get some ice cream?"

"Hey! No," Jeff said, looking in and smiling at Ally and Nick. "I've got to finish what I'm doing. Working on a project."

"What project?" Ally asked.

"A surprise for Coombsie and my aunt. Do you know he's been down there all day, every day, since the other night?"

"Sounds like those two might be an item," Mrs. O'Connor said.

"Yeah, right," Jeff snorted.

"Why not?" Ally said. "They make a good couple."

"Whatever."

"Well, you'd be surprised," Mrs. O'Connor said. "Give it a chance."

"Yeah, I guess."

"Good. We'll see you later."

"Yeah, see you later, Jeff," Ally called.

Mr. O'Connor pulled away from him, and soon they were zooming down the road toward town.

The family spent the evening at a local bookstore and then went to the ice cream shop. They returned home at 9:15. As Mr. O'Connor turned onto their road, they all noticed the police cars, their emergency lights twirling.

"What's going on?" Mr. O'Connor asked as they drove closer to several police cars stopped in front of a house. Ally's heart pounded, and she prayed that whatever it was didn't involve Jeff.

When they reached the cars, Ally spotted Mr. Bell. Mr. O'Connor rolled down the window, and Mr. Bell stepped over to it.

"Something going on?" Mr. O'Connor asked.

"Yeah, I'll tell you later," Mr. Bell said. "But they think they have the guy."

Ally looked around the area, but saw no sign of Jeff or anyone else she knew. Mr. O'Connor drove on to Nick's house, and Ally got out and walked Nick to his front door.

"Do you think they got Jeff?" Nick said as he opened the door.

Ally felt close to tears. "This is horrible, just horrible. Pray, okay. Just promise me you'll pray."

"I will. I am right now."

Ally returned to the car, and Mr. O'Connor drove home. Once there, Ally sat on the front porch, praying, while her parents went inside. She felt guilty for not having warned Jeff, and guilty for not making him tell the truth, and guilty for everything else. *Why didn't I have more courage?*

Minutes later, she heard footsteps. A figure came into the light of the porch. It was Coombsie. He looked nervous and worried.

"Ally, do you know where Jeff is? Babs is worried."

"The police haven't called her?" Ally asked.

"The police? No, no one had called when I left fifteen minutes ago."

Ally jumped up. "The tree fort!"

"Let's go."

Ally ran in to tell her parents she had to go out for a little while. Mrs. O'Connor protested, but when she saw Coombsie, she said, "Is something wrong?"

"Jeff has disappeared," Coombsie said.

"Should we call the police?"

"No, I think I know where he is," Ally said. "Can I call Nick and get him to come with us?"

"I guess. It's kind of late, though."

"Coombsie'll be with us."

"Okay. I guess so. But don't be too long."

Ally called Nick, and soon all three of them were headed for the tree fort, their flashlights lit up.

They found the tree fort and saw a light on in it. Ally sighed with relief. At least Jeff hadn't been nabbed by the police.

As they approached the fort, Jeff looked out the window. "I knew it!" he cried. "You followed me!"

"Jeff, what's going on?" Ally said.

Coombsie added, "Your auntie is worried sick, Jeff."

"No," Jeff said, standing in the window. "You followed me! I saw your tracks in the dirt, and you came up here, didn't you? You were in my private place without asking."

Ally tried to reason with him. "Jeff, we just—"

"I can't trust anyone, anywhere. Everyone is a snitch! Get away! Get away from me! You're all traitors."

"Jeff, what's going on?" Coombsie said. "Is this about your father?"

"I can't believe you did this to me, Coombsie. I thought we were friends."

"Did you get the electronic equipment at the dump?" Ally asked.

"Where else? You still think I'm the one trashing the houses, don't you? All of you? Don't you?"

Ally said, "Jeff, maybe if we all go back to the house, we can talk this out."

"No, I'm through with it. I'm getting out of here. The only thing I'm doing with you is the carnival tomorrow, and then I'm done with you all."

Jeff climbed down the rope ladder and stormed down the trail. Ally started after him, but Coombsie grabbed her shoulder. "He'll cool down. Give him a night. I'll talk to him in the morning."

When Jeff's flashlight beam had disappeared among the trees, Coombsie turned to Nick and Ally. "He has this cock-

90

eyed idea of saving his father and getting him out of prison. I've tried to talk him out of it hundreds of times. But he thought if he got someone to fix the electronic equipment, he could get enough money to hire a lawyer. It was crazy, plumb crazy."

"It's all right. It's my fault," Ally said. "I'm the one who's been spying on him and thinking he was wrecking the houses and stealing the equipment."

"Why didn't you ask me? I was sure he was getting it from the dump."

"I was afraid."

"Of what?"

Ally glanced uneasily at Nick. "That he . . . I don't know . . . that everyone would think me stupid and that Jeff would do exactly what he's done—think I betrayed him."

"Ally, you can't save people with wrong information," Coombsie said. "And only Jesus can save people to begin with."

"You're a Christian, Coombsie?"

"Until I met Babs, a pretty bitter one. But God's done a lot of work in the last few days."

"Coombsie, is Jeff a Christian?" Ally asked.

"Oh, I've been talking to him about it. But no, I don't think so. That's one of the things he doesn't like about Babs. She's always telling him he needs Jesus!"

Ally suddenly burst into tears. "I've blown it. I've blown everything."

Coombsie wrapped his huge arms around her for a second. "Don't worry, little one. God works things for good in our lives, right? He'll work this for good too."

"But Jeff thinks I'm a traitor."

"You only wanted to help him, Ally," Coombsie said. "He'll see that tomorrow."

"I hope so."

"Come on, let's go home."

Sixteen

A Little Fun

The next morning, Ally connected with Nick, and they both headed down to Jeff's house. Ally's parents and Nick's family were planning to arrive at the carnival later, when the talent show started. But Jeff had wanted to get there early so Ally and Nick could see the arena where they'd be performing.

Ally had worried all night about whether or not Jeff would still be angry. She hoped Coombsie had talked to him.

When they arrived at Miss Kruck's house, they were greeted by Jeff saying, "You're late."

"Sorry. We had a late night," Ally said, biting her tongue. She tried to get Jeff to look her in the eye, but he stood with his shoulders hunched, looking at the ground.

"Do you have the costume?" Ally asked.

Miss Kruck answered, "Everything's in the car. Come on. Your parents will get there later?"

"Yeah, after we've practiced. We are going to practice, aren't we, Jeff?"

"Whatever."

Miss Kruck sighed. "Jeff, Ally is your friend. Please try to treat her as such."

Jeff rolled his eyes and opened the car door. Everyone piled in and settled down, Ally and Nick in the back and Miss Kruck and Jeff up front.

"Come on, Jeff, perk up! This is going to be fun," Miss Kruck said. "Now where do we pick up Mr. Coombs?"

"Up the road a bit."

Miss Kruck drove down the main street, then turned on the highway. A couple of miles down they saw Coombsie standing by the road.

Miss Kruck stopped, and Coombsie got in the back.

"Is everybody ready to win?" he asked as he hopped in.

Ally and Nick nodded, but Jeff didn't acknowledge the question. Miss Kruck then looked at Coombsie through the rearview mirror.

"Lovely to see you, Nestor."

"Nestor!?" Ally and Nick exclaimed.

Coombsie sank down in his seat a bit and made a face.

"It's his name, for heaven's sake," Miss Kruck explained. "I'm not going to call him Coombsie."

Jeff murmured, "Why not? I like it better."

Miss Kruck ignored Jeff's bad attitude. She looked in her rearview mirror again. "Nestor, how would you like to go shopping tonight after the carnival? You, me, and Jeff could all go together. We could find you a nice shirt to wear to church on Sunday."

"Church!" Jeff cried out in dismay.

"And a new pair of pants and socks and shoes," Coombsie said with enthusiasm. "Got to look good for the preacher."

Jeff frowned and turned back to regard his friend. "I don't believe this. Pretty soon you'll be civilized, Coombsie."

"I hope not. I like him just the way he is," Miss Kruck said with a smile.

"Oh man, what has happened to everyone?" Jeff moaned.

Miss Kruck didn't respond, but just turned into the parking lot for the carnival fairgrounds.

Jeff, Nick, and Ally unloaded everything and looked for signs to the arena. After walking a while in silence, Ally ventured, "Jeff, I'm sorry—"

"Don't apologize. I don't want to talk about it."

"But we were so afraid the police had . . ."

"Had what?"

"The police and Mr. Bell—we saw them last night, talking about catching someone."

"So? Let's just do our thing and then go our separate ways, okay?"

"Look, I made a mistake. But I was just trying to stop you from doing what I thought might be something bad. Is that so wrong?"

"People should trust each other," Jeff said and turned away, walking a little faster than Nick and Ally.

After they had practiced, Jeff split off from Ally and Nick to get something to eat. He said he wanted to be alone, so Ally and Nick walked around, looking at the exhibits and other events.

When it came time for their performance, Ally saw her family with the Parkers and Miss Kruck and Coombsie in the stands. Various acts went on, but finally the announcer's voice reeled off their act.

"And now, Jeff Reynolds, Ally O'Connor, and Nick Parker will give us their rendition of a knight and his gentle horse, Delilah."

Ally and Nick rattled out into the arena, bumping and shifting, provoking laughter from the crowd. They both had remote microphones on their shirts so their voices could be heard. Nick neighed up in the front, led Ally over to the crowd, and tried to grab a candy apple from a kid. This brought more laughter.

Finally Jeff stepped out in his knight outfit. He was wearing a helmet and had a sword at his side. He looked like a

94

real knight, until he started toward the horse. Then his feet became rubber; he had a hard time standing up, and he fell on his behind several times. That ignited more laughter. Jeff stood up, brushed himself off. Nick and Ally made their neighing noises sound like laughter, and this really got the crowd going.

Jeff then tried to run after the horse, but Ally and Nick sidewinded out of the way, throwing Jeff to the mat. By now, the place was in an uproar.

The routine went on for about five minutes, until Jeff said, "My people, methinks I will get me a new horse. And new legs. New boots. A new mind and a new life. And a new behind."

This brought down the house. Everyone agreed the routine was the best they'd seen that day, and Ally, Nick, and Jeff won the contest.

Afterwards, Nick and Ally walked around, greeting people and receiving compliments. Jeff, though, disappeared in the dressing rooms, and Ally didn't see him for nearly an hour.

Later Ally found him playing a game in which you threw three balls at three stacked solid-metal milk bottles. Ally walked over to him and said, "Winning a doll for somebody?"

"Nobody I know of," Jeff said when he knocked over all three milk bottles and won a stuffed bear. He promptly gave it to a little girl passing by with her parents.

"Jeff," Ally said, beginning to feel angry, "can you just forgive me, or is that too much to ask?"

"God'll forgive you if you beg him enough," Jeff said. "But not me. I'm not God."

"Jeff, I was only thinking of what was best for you."

"Sure you were. Do you want to burp me and change my diaper too?"

"That's not fair."

Jeff eyed her angrily. "I suppose you're going to tell me I should accept Jesus so I can forgive you, so I can become a good Christian. Like Coombsie and my aunt and everybody I seem to know is. Is that it?"

"Accepting Jesus means that *you're* forgiven," Ally blurted.

"Maybe I don't want to be forgiven," Jeff said icily. "Maybe I haven't done anything."

Ally turned to Nick, who stood at her side. "Come on, let's go find our families."

As they walked off, Ally turned and saw Jeff standing alone, looking like he was glad to see her go.

"I don't know what to do, Nick."

"Let him ride it out. He needs some air, that's all."

Tears burned in Ally's eyes. "I blew it. I blew everything. And now he hates me."

"He doesn't hate you," Nick said. "He just doesn't like you very much at the moment."

"Thanks."

"Come on," Nick said, giving her a little punch on the upper arm. "It'll be okay."

"I sure hope so."

They found their families sitting at an ice cream stand with Miss Kruck and Coombsie.

"Hey," Miss Kruck said, "why don't you all come to my place, and we'll have a nice steak dinner?"

Mrs. O'Connor answered for everyone. "We'd love to."

Jeff suddenly appeared at the edge of the tent, and Coombsie walked over to him and put his hand on his shoulder. "Babs and I'll take Jeff home. We'll see you all at 6:00."

Seventeen

A Clever Story

Coombsie played his violin for the O'Connors and the Parkers while Ally helped Miss Kruck prepare dinner in the kitchen. Jeff looked uncomfortable and didn't say much.

"Miss Kruck, do you think Jeff hates me now?" Ally asked.

"Honey, don't worry about it. Jeff'll get over it eventually."

"I'm sorry I messed everything up."

"Hey, you were just trying to help him," Miss Kruck said. "Jeff has to learn that when people try to help him, however they do it, they do it because they care about him. He simply doesn't think anyone cares."

"I only wish he would figure out that we all care. I thought today would really have gotten him feeling better. We did such a good job on the skit, but he seems more down than ever."

"Pray for him, honey. That's all I know to do. I've been doing it for all of his fourteen years now," Miss Kruck said as she cut the large T-bone steaks into smaller pieces.

Ally was quiet for a moment; then her curiosity got the better of her. "By the way, I thought Jeff's father is your brother."

"That's right."

"Then why isn't your last name the same as Jeff's?"

"Well, Jeff's dad changed it when he left on his own the first time. Jeff got his new name. It's better than Kruck, I think." She laughed. "We always took a lot of flack about our name growing up. It was very hard on Jeff's dad. He hated it and couldn't wait to change it the first chance he had." Miss Kruck finished cutting the steaks. "Well, dinner's ready. Come on, let's serve it."

So Ally and Miss Kruck marched plates in hand, and everyone retired to the dining room. After Coombsie said grace, everyone dug in. The meal was delicious, with Chinese string beans, steak, and fried potatoes and onions. The conversation went nicely, but Ally kept noticing that Jeff ate in silence.

When everyone finished, Ally said, "Do you have a new story, Coombsie?"

"Oh, I shouldn't bore everyone with it."

"It won't be boring," Ally said. "Mom and Dad, you should hear this."

"Okay, it's a love story," Coombsie said, clearly relishing the spotlight.

"Tell it! Tell it!" Ally said, hoping the story would snap Jeff into a better mood.

"It's very short," Coombsie said. "This is it. The pauper was out on the street, and the princess went by. He saw she was about to step in a mud puddle, so he pulled out his violin case and laid it down for her to cross the mud puddle. The princess slipped as she walked across. But the pauper grabbed her and held her. Their faces came together.

And he said, 'I'd ask you to marry me, but I'm just a pauper.' And she said, 'I have enough riches for both of us.' She took out her purse and showed him. Then he took out his wallet. A butterfly flew out. The princess caught it and let it land on the end of her finger. 'What does this mean?' she asked. 'A free creature has come into the circle of your love,' the pauper replied, 'and he will remain there forever.' And then they lived happily ever after!"

"Cool!" Ally said.

"Oh, that was just wonderful," Jeff said sarcastically. He looked at his aunt. "I suppose you almost stepped in a mud puddle today at the carnival."

Miss Kruck sighed. "Jeff, I know you're upset, but can you please try to be happy for us?"

Jeff stood up. "If everyone's so happy, fine. I'll just be myself."

With that he left the table.

Jeff's exit put a damper on the whole evening. The O'Connors and the Parkers left soon after.

When Ally settled down for the night in her room, her mom stepped in to kiss her good night.

"It was a good day, Mom, even with Jeff being out of sorts."

"The best," Mrs. O'Connor answered, her eyes fixed on Ally's. "Don't worry about Jeff. He's resilient."

"I just wish he could be happy for Miss Kruck and Coombsie," Ally said, slipping deeper under the covers. "You think they'll get married, Mom?"

"Well, honey," Ally's mom said, laughing, "I think it's a little too soon to tell. After all, they just met. But I hope they have a future together, for Jeff's sake. It might really help him settle in for once."

"Yeah, that's what I think."

Mrs. O'Connor kissed Ally, then turned out the light. "Love ya."

"Love ya back."

Mrs. O'Connor stepped out into the hall and closed Ally's door behind her.

Missing in Action

Early the next morning, Ally was awakened by the telephone. She rolled over and picked up the phone on her bedstand.

"Hello?" she said groggily.

"Hello? Is this Ally?"

"Yes."

The voice on the other end paused. "Ally, this is Miss Kruck. I apologize for calling so early, but I wanted to know if you've seen Jeff since last night."

"No, I haven't. Why do you ask?" Ally said, concerned.

"I'm just so worried! He must've left before dawn. I'm afraid of what he might be doing or what might've happened to him."

"Have you called the police?"

Miss Kruck sniffled. "No, it's too soon to do that. But I've contacted Mr. Coombs, and we're going to go look for him."

"I'm coming too!" Ally said.

"I don't know," Miss Kruck said with uncertainty.

"I really want to come!" Ally argued. "Let me get dressed and tell my parents. I'll meet you over at your house."

"Well, all right then. I'll see you in a few minutes," Miss Kruck said and then hung up.

Ally hurriedly threw on some clothes, rushed to her parents' room, and knocked on the door.

"Yes?" Mrs. O'Connor's voice rang out.

Ally stepped inside. "Mom, Jeff is missing. Miss Kruck is afraid he's doing something crazy."

"What do you want us to do, honey?"

"Nothing. But I want to go with her and Coombsie to look for him."

Mrs. O'Connor looked at Mr. O'Connor. He nodded his head.

"All right, Ally, you can go. But I'm coming with you."

"And I'll stay at home, in case Jeff shows up here," Mrs. O'Connor added.

Before Ally and her father left the house, Ally called Nick, and they picked him up on the way to Miss Kruck's. When they arrived, Coombsie and Miss Kruck were standing out in front of the house.

"Do you know where Jeff could've gone?" Coombsie asked. "He was always telling me he was getting ready to do something, but he never said what. Something about his father is all I can figure."

"Did anyone look in the tree fort?" Ally suggested.

"Well, it's a good place to start," Coombsie said. "I walked by there last night on my way home and he wasn't there. But maybe he is now."

Everyone hopped into Mr. O'Connor's car.

"I should never have spied on him," Ally said, feeling close to tears. "I should have known he wasn't stealing the stuff from the houses. But all that electronic stuff at the tree fort . . ."

"Yeah, he got it all at the dump," Coombsie said. "He thought he could repair them and sell them and help get his father a decent lawyer to spring him out of jail."

"Speaking of the thefts, did you know they caught who was doing it?" Mr. O'Connor said.

Everyone turned to him as he put the car in gear and started up the road.

"Who is it?" Ally asked.

"Bell. It was Mr. Bell," Mr. O'Connor said. "He was tearing the places up to get the insurance money. Mr. Coombs found out yesterday while you three kids were at the carnival."

"Why didn't you tell us?" Ally said incredulously.

"Plumb forgot in all the excitement," Coombsie said.

"How did you find out it was him?"

"Was tracking him for awhile. I knew they might try to pin it on Jeff. So I decided to check it out for myself. Finally made heads and tails of it."

"You were tracking us too, weren't you?" Ally said. "Like when you stopped Jeff from going into the tree fort when we were in it."

"Just helping out," Coombsie said. "Woods can be dangerous. The stray dogs from the dump can be kind of wild."

"Stop here, Dad," Ally said. "This is the way to the tree fort."

Mr. O'Connor hit the brakes and soon most of them were hiking down the trail to the tree fort. Mr. O'Connor stayed in the car in case he saw Jeff on the road.

At the tree fort, Ally and Nick climbed up the ladder and looked at the items inside. Everything looked like it usually did.

Ally stepped to the window.

"Everything's here, I think," she called down to Miss Kruck and Coombsie.

Nick rubbed his chin, studying the layout of the tree fort. "Some things are gone," he said.

"What?" Ally asked.

"His backpack is missing."

She leaned out the window again. "Jeff's backpack is gone. What do you think is going on?"

"He was always talking about getting to his father in prison," Coombsie said. "He was obsessed with it."

"And I wouldn't take him because I didn't want him to find out the awful truth," Miss Kruck added.

"The awful truth?"

"Jeff's father isn't just in prison. He's is in a psychiatric facility for the criminally insane," Miss Kruck answered. "I didn't want to let Jeff see his father like that. It's my fault. I should have told him."

As Ally and Nick stepped down the ladder to the ground, Ally asked, "How was Jeff going to visit his father, Coombsie? He's only fourteen. He can't drive a car."

"I don't know. He never told me."

Nick snapped his fingers. "I know what else is missing up there."

"What?" everyone asked at once.

"The bag of oats."

Ally covered her mouth. "The horses. He's gone for the horses."

"Let's go," Coombsie said, "before he becomes a horse thief."

Nineteen

At the Farm

When they got back to Mr. O'Connor in the car, everyone was talking at once, but Ally climbed into the front seat and told her father they were heading for Mrs. Hanson's farm.

Mr. O'Connor careened down the road and at Ally and Nick's directions, turned off to the dirt road back to the farm.

They reached the farm and parked. All was quiet until Jeff burst from the barn, riding Thunder. He was wearing his backpack, and the horse had pack saddles on it. When Jeff saw everyone, he wheeled and shot out off across the field.

"Jeff, stop!" Miss Kruck called.

Mrs. Hanson ran out of her house. "I heard something. What's going on?" she yelled.

"Jeff took Thunder!" Ally said. "He's galloping across the meadow."

"We can head him off on the road to the dump," Coombsie said. "If he goes that way."

"It's dangerous with those dogs," Mrs. Hanson said. "And Thunder has been crazy this week. He's lathered up

105

for a ride. You've got to stop Jeff. That horse will kill him if he starts jumping fences."

Ally looked at Coombsie. "I know what to do. Nick and I can get on two of the other horses and follow him. Coombsie can lead Dad around by the dump."

"Go!" Coombsie said. "If that horse gets out of control, Jeff'll fall off. He's not that good of a rider."

"Okay," Ally yelled as she ran toward the barn.

In minutes, she and Nick had Snowbird and Lucky saddled up. They roared out of the barn just as Mr. O'Connor shot out of the farmyard with Coombsie and Miss Kruck in the car.

Ally and Nick galloped up the road to the first path in between the fields where they'd last seen Jeff. The tracks of his horse could be clearly seen. Ally slowed down to a loping pace, watching the tracks. She and Nick reached the edge of the field and found a road she'd never been on.

"Where does this go?" she asked, looking both ways.

Nick studied the landscape. "He went to the left. Look!"

The pair of saddlebags Jeff had put on Thunder lay in the dirt about ten yards up the road.

"Go!" Ally said, kicking Snowbird and clucking.

They raced up the road. Coming around a corner, they saw Jeff stopped in the road about a hundred yards ahead. He had climbed down off Thunder and was picking something up in the road.

"Jeff, stop!" Ally cried.

Jeff didn't acknowledge Ally's call, but got back on Thunder and stormed down the road at a pace Ally was almost afraid to keep up. She pushed Snowbird into an all-out gallop. Nick was right beside her, leaning forward on Lucky and gripping the horn of the saddle.

"We can catch him, I think," Ally cried above the pounding of the hooves.

"Thunder's a thoroughbred," Nick yelled back. "Are you crazy?"

"Just try, okay?"

Ally's knees ached as she gripped the saddle with her legs. The horses' panting came in great chuffs. She knew Snowbird would be worn out in a matter of minutes.

As Ally pushed the horse even harder, Jeff slowed ahead and turned to the right.

"He's going around the dump," Nick yelled.

"Maybe Dad will be there."

Jeff disappeared, and as Ally and Nick came up on the turn, they slowed down. The warm air burned Ally's throat. She was panting, and her arms were tired from reining Snowbird.

They made the turn and cantered down the road toward the dump, Jeff in full sight ahead of them.

"We can't keep this up, Ally," Nick shouted.

"Just a few more minutes and we can get to him, I think," Ally answered. "There's not many places to go at the dump, remember? Just around it."

Jeff veered off to the left around the huge pit of the dump. Ally watched as he galloped into the main area.

At the same moment, she saw her dad, Coombsie, Miss Kruck, and Mrs. Hanson run out from the car, yelling and gesticulating to Jeff. He ignored them and took the road around and behind the dump.

Ally knew she had to rest, so she and Nick pulled up and stopped in front of her dad and the others.

"We can't catch him," she said, huffing hard.

"Where can he go from the dump, Coombsie?" Nick asked, panting hard too.

"The road back there comes out near that farm that was burned out," Coombsie answered.

"That's just down the street from our house," Mr. O'Connor said.

"Why would Jeff go there?" Miss Kruck asked.

"Maybe he has another stash there," Coombsie said. "He told me once that he had a knife and some other things he thought would help him with his father. But I never saw any of those things in the tree fort."

"Is there a shorter way, Coombsie?" Ally asked. "These horses are almost beat."

"Yeah, on the right side of the dump, there's another trail through the trees that goes behind the houses. You come out just below your home road."

"Let's try it," Ally said.

"We'll meet you at the farm. Be careful!" Mr. O'Connor added.

Ally and Nick started off down the dirt road to the right of the dump. "The horses will get some rest if we go fairly slow," Ally told Nick. So they loped down the wide trail that had been made, apparently, for equipment to tear down the trees in the development. It was slow going. Ally just hoped they would arrive in time to keep Jeff from getting into any trouble with the authorities.

Twenty

Disaster

Ally and Nick came out of the trail just above the Matthews's farm. They turned in the direction of the farm. Seconds later, they saw Jeff hurtle down the road on Thunder with six angry dogs chasing him.

"Dump dogs!" Nick said with horror.

Ally was about to kick Snowbird into a full gallop again when Jeff suddenly jerked Thunder up short. The horse wheeled and looked like it would fall over. Then the dump dogs raced up, snapping at the horse's heels. Thunder reared up on his hind legs, and Jeff tumbled backwards.

A second later, Thunder jolted forward, but Jeff was no longer astride.

Ally clucked Snowbird, hoping Jeff wasn't hurt from the fall.

Moments later, she saw that Jeff's right foot was caught in the stirrup. Thunder was dragging him on his back up the road! The dump dogs' barking had spooked the horse into a full gallop.

"No!" Ally shrieked and shot after the horse, who was now careening up what had once been the Matthews's driveway. Nick galloped alongside Ally after Thunder and

Jeff. It looked to Ally like Jeff wasn't even trying to get loose.

Then she realized he must have been knocked out.

She and Nick gained on Thunder, and in another half minute they were alongside the big horse. Ally hardly noticed that the dump dogs had run back into the trees. But she did see that Thunder's reins were flying free. She had to grab them. At a full gallop, she reached across the space between the two horses, being careful not to trample Jeff. But the thought of grabbing the reins terrified her. There was no way she could do it. She reached again and almost fell off Snowbird.

"You can't do it," Nick shouted.

There had to be a way.

Ahead of them, the Matthews's pond sparkled in the sunlight.

"Go on the other side," she yelled to Nick. "Maybe we can block Thunder into stopping."

Nick slowed and came up on the other side. They were less than a hundred yards away from the pond. Jeff hadn't cried out, though Ally hadn't had a chance to get a good look, she knew he must be unconscious.

She pressed Snowbird close to the big thoroughbred. What was Thunder going for? Then, Ally remembered Mrs. Hanson saying something about the horse liking to cool off in the pond. If the horse went in, Jeff could drown.

Nick had come up on the other side of Thunder, galloping neck and neck. Ally felt her arms pounding with adrenaline. It was now or never.

"Squeeze in!" she shouted.

Nick brought Lucky closer to Thunder and then ahead of him. Ally forced Snowbird far enough ahead not to stomp on Jeff and closed in.

"Please, Lord, do something!" Ally prayed in her mind. "Don't let Jeff die!"

The two horses pinioned Thunder between them.

"Slow down now!" Ally yelled.

Nick slowed and so did Ally. Thunder was forced to slow himself.

As the seconds ticked off, they came closer and closer to the pond. Thunder slowed even more until, moments later, the three horses came to a stop.

Ally sighed with relief. "Grab the reins," she said to Nick as she climbed off Snowbird. She came around behind Snowbird and grasped Jeff's boot. She looked at his face, but his eyes were closed.

"Please don't be dead," she murmured desperately.

The boot was stuck. "Come on!" she cried.

Ally didn't see it coming.

The dump dogs charged out of the trees again. Thunder reared, then bolted forward into the pond, still dragging Jeff.

Twenty-one

Double Disaster

Snowbird and Lucky leaped away from the dogs and galloped off toward the burned-out house. Ally stared in horror as Thunder began swimming about. Jeff was completely submerged under the water.

Ally didn't wait. She dove into the pond and swam after the horse as quickly as she could. Fortunately, in the water Thunder was slow, and Ally reached him in seconds. She ducked under the water and grabbed Jeff's boot, which was still caught in the stirrup. But she couldn't seem to release it. "Please God," she screamed in her mind. "Do something!"

She suddenly felt someone behind her.

It was Coombsie. He dove under her and released the saddle. The whole thing came off. Ally pulled Jeff to the surface, and she and Coombsie drew him and the saddle toward shore.

Seconds later, they pulled Jeff out. He was unconscious, his back and head beaten up from being dragged so far. Coombsie administered CPR, with Mr. O'Connor working on Jeff's heart.

Seconds later, Jeff sputtered air but didn't open his eyes.

"He's breathing! He's breathing!" Coombsie yelled.

"Let's get him to the hospital," Mr. O'Connor said, darting off after his car.

❧

Ally sat by Jeff's hospital bed, with Nick, Coombsie, Miss Kruck, and the O'Connors looking on. Jeff's face was battered, both eyes black and lips torn up. He had not suffered a neck or spine injury, though. No bones broken. That was the miracle. But now he lay in a coma, giving no sign of understanding or even a flicker of consciousness.

Over the next several days, Ally, Coombsie, and Miss Kruck took turns sitting by Jeff's bed. Ally read to him from comic books, *Sports Illustrated*—anything she thought might interest him. Coombsie brought in his violin and played for hours at a time. Miss Kruck was nearly distraught with worry, so she and Ally prayed together frequently.

Then school started, but Ally went through her classes listlessly, not paying attention, thinking constantly about Jeff.

The only one who was upbeat was Nick. He clowned around and tried to get Jeff to respond to his jokes.

Jeff didn't flicker an eyelash.

After Jeff had been in a coma for a week, everyone began to lose heart. Ally came in one night after spending some time out at the Hanson farm. Mrs. Hanson came by the hospital several times, but that evening Ally was the only one present. She spent the first few minutes in silent prayer, then took Jeff's hand and prayed out loud.

When she could think of nothing more to pray, she told Jeff about school, her friends, the teachers. Coombsie and Miss Kruck stepped into the room at 7:00, carrying both of their violins. When they began to play, nurses in the hall stopped in to listen.

Jeff still didn't move.

Coombsie launched into a long rendition of "Are You Sleeping, Brother John," and other tunes he thought up off the cuff. Miss Kruck sat down, once again near tears. She said to Ally, "It's all my fault. I should have told him about his father long ago. I just didn't have the heart. He idolized the man so, for reasons I've never understood."

Ally took her hand and said, "I think Jeff would understand."

Finally, Coombsie stopped playing and launched into a story. Ally listened, praying while Coombsie talked quietly next to Jeff on the opposite side of the bed.

"It's about our little dog family this time," Coombsie said. "I've got all the puppies placed except one, and that one's for you. You'll have to take good care of him because he comes from a long line—"

Ally suddenly noticed Jeff's hand twitching. She grabbed it and pressed on the fingers. "That's it. Feel that? That's us. Come back to us, Jeff. Please come back."

The hand twitched some more, then the feet.

Coombsie stood and picked up his violin. "Come to the music, boy. Come to the music." He began playing vigorously.

Miss Kruck grabbed Jeff's feet and shook them. "There!" she said. "Feel that! You feel that! Then knock out of this thing!"

Jeff's eyes popped open.

Twenty-two

Back

The moment he awoke, Jeff smiled beautifully, looking at Ally, then at Miss Kruck, and finally at Coombsie.

"Where am I?" he asked.

"In the hospital," Miss Kruck said. "You fell off Thunder at the burned-out farm, but your foot was caught in the stirrup. The horse dragged you a long ways."

Jeff felt around the gauze and bandages. "I'm pretty beat up, huh?"

"Yeah."

"Don't talk, Jeff," Coombsie said. "Just rest."

Jeff laid back on the pillows as everyone filled him in on all that had happened since the accident. Soon visiting hours were over, and everyone had to go home. But the next evening, the whole crew showed up to see him.

When Ally and her parents arrived, Jeff was eager to talk. He turned to Ally. "I guess I kind of blew it, didn't I?"

"No, it wasn't you who blew it," Ally said. "It was me. Just let me apologize. I'm sorry about everything. I was wrong. I should have believed you."

"Hey, it's okay," Jeff said. "I'm not always very trustworthy." He grinned, then turned to Miss Kruck. "But I'm beginning to know who is. When I fell off Thunder and realized my foot was caught in the stirrup, I prayed, 'Jesus, you have to help me.' Then Thunder took off, and I was bumping along. I didn't feel saved, but a funny thing happened—I had this sense like I was being lifted up, like Jesus was right there. It was amazing."

"You felt like Jesus was there with you?"

"Yeah. I didn't see him or anything. I just knew."

"That's what it is," Miss Kruck said. "You just know."

Coombsie took out his violin. "I think it's appropriate that I play something appropriate." Then he began playing a heartrending version of "Amazing Grace."

When Coombsie was done, Jeff said, "I don't know what it is. Nothing's really changed . . . except something in me . . . and I feel happy for the first time in my whole life."

"Jesus joy," Coombsie said. "That's what I got back when I met Babs."

Miss Kruck smiled.

"Are you getting married?" Jeff asked hesitantly.

Coombsie and Miss Kruck laughed. "I think it's a bit too soon for that," Coombsie said. "But we sure would like to get to know each other better. If that's okay with you."

"Yeah, that's okay with me."

Everyone was quiet a moment, then Jeff said, "By the way, how's Thunder?"

"Covered in blankets, sitting by a fire and sipping hot oat mash," Ally said.

"Is Mrs. Hanson mad at me?"

Mr. O'Connor said, "She's just glad you're okay."

"I'll have to go over and apologize."

Then a nurse came in and told them visiting hours were almost over. The gang left, but Ally stayed behind for a minute. It was the first she'd been alone with Jeff since he'd awakened.

"So, I guess we'll be going to school together," Jeff said.

116

"Yeah. Maybe we'll even have some of the same teachers, but I don't know your schedule."

"So when will I be able to go out on a real date with you?"

"I'll discuss it when I'm sixteen."

"Is that what you tell Nick?"

"Always."

"So it'll be him against me?"

Ally grinned. "I wouldn't think of it that way. I want you and Nick to be friends."

"I guess I can do that. Nick's a cool guy." Jeff touched Ally's hand. "But we would make a great couple, you know."

"When I'm sixteen, we'll talk about it."

"Till then, we'll just be friends, right?"

"Yeah. Great friends. Best friends."

"Really?"

"Sure."

"I guess I can deal with that."

Ally gave Jeff's hand a squeeze. "See you, pardner. I've got to get going."

"Yeah, see you later, Ally."

When Ally and her parents got home that night, Mrs. O'Connor said, "That's an amazing story about Jeff accepting Jesus, you know."

"I know. Do you think it's real?" Ally asked.

"Only time will tell. But it's a good start." Mrs. O'Connor smiled. "You did good, Ally."

"What did I do?"

"You saved Jeff's life, in more ways than one."

"I didn't do it."

"You and God and Nick and everyone. God used everyone."

They stepped into the house, and a little puppy ran up to greet them. A moment later, Shea came around the corner. Ally picked up the puppy and nuzzled it. "I'm glad

Coombsie let Jasper stay here until Jeff comes home," Ally said. "Somehow a puppy gives you peace."

Mrs. O'Connor pet Shea. "I'm glad Coombsie let us take Shea. She's a good dog. Aren't you, girl?"

Shea barked happily.

Ally set the puppy down to romp. "I think God is good even when it looks bad, Mom. Don't you think?"

"Always, honey. Always."

Mark Littleton, a former pastor and youth pastor, is a writer and a speaker at churches, retreats, conferences, and other Christian gatherings. He is happily married to Jeanette Gardner and has three children, Nicole, Alisha, and Gardner, also known as Gard-zilla the Destroyer because, at three years old, he is able to destroy whole cities when left unattended for more than thirty seconds. Mark and his family have a dog named Patches and a cat named Beauty, who is afraid of the dog. Mark collects lighthouses, original paintings of ships, and hundred dollar bills. He is willing to add any contributions you might wish to make to his collections, especially the hundred dollar bill collection.

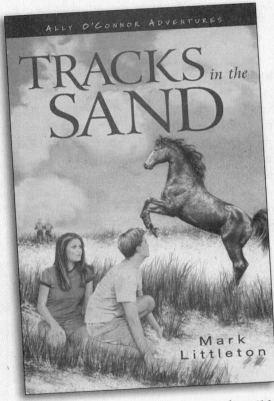

ALLY O'CONNOR ADVENTURES

TRACKS *in the* SAND

Mark Littleton

BOOK 1
TRACKS *in the* SAND

It's summer break, and 14-year-old Ally and her best friend Nick are vacationing with their families at North Carolina's Outer Banks. Ally, Nick, and their three other friends have heard stories about the wild mustangs roaming the protected wildlife area on the island. This visit, they're determined to catch a glimpse of the majestic horses.

But Ally and Nick soon discover someone else is tracking the horses, too. Who are these two mean-sounding men? And is that a rifle one of them is carrying? As Ally, Nick, and the others search for answers, they find themselves in a dangerous situation. Now they must not only rescue the wild mustangs—but each other!

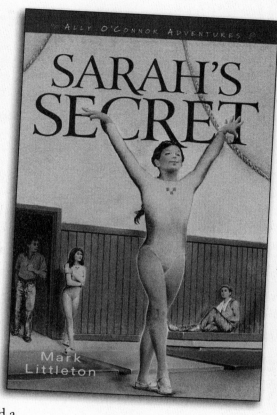

BOOK 2
SARAH'S SECRET

Sarah Matthews is the new girl in town. She's also the most talented performer in Ally O'Connor's gymnastics class—and the team's best hope for winning at competition. As Nick, Molly, Ally, and John begin to build a friendship with Sarah, they discover there are serious problems in her home.

Sarah's dad is controlling and abusive. He seems to care only about his thoroughbred horse, Colonel, and that Sarah gets her chores done. When he forbids Sarah to compete as a gymnast, Ally and friends come up with a plan to change his mind. Things begin to improve with the help of Coach James, until Mr. Matthews loses control. With her and her mother's life at risk, will Sarah have the courage to tell the truth?